A VILLAGE OF VAGABONDS

A VILLAGE OF VAGABONDS

By F. BERKELEY SMITH

Author of "The Lady of Big Shanty,"

A. L. BURT COMPANY

PUBLISHERS   NEW YORK

CONTENTS

A VILLAGE OF VAGABONDS

A Village of Vagabonds

CHAPTER ONE

THE HOUSE BY THE MARSH

IT WAS in fat Madame Fontaine's little café
at Bar la Rose, that Norman village by
the sea, that I announced my decision. It
being market-day the café was noisy with
peasants, and the crooked street without jammed
with carts. Monsieur Torin, the butcher, opposite me, leaned back heavily from his glass of
applejack and roared.

Monsieur Pompanet, the blacksmith, at my
elbow, put down his cup of black coffee delicately
in its clean saucer and opened his honest
gray eyes wide in amazement. Simultaneously
Monsieur Jaclin, the mayor, in his freshly

ironed blouse, who for want of room was squeezed next to Torin, choked out a wheezy "*Bon Dieu!*" and blew his nose in derision.

"Pont du Sable — *Bon Dieu!*" exclaimed all three. "Pont du Sable — *Bon Dieu!*"

"*Cristi!*" thundered Torin. "You say you are going to *live* in Pont du Sable? *Hélas!* It is not possible, my friend, you are in earnest!"

"That lost hole of a village of *sacré* vagabonds," echoed Pompanet. "Why, the mud when the tide is out smells like the devil. It is unhealthy."

"Père Bordier and I went there for ducks twenty years ago," added the mayor. "We were glad enough to get away before dark. B-r-r! It was lonely enough, that marsh, and that dirty little fishing-village no longer than your arm. Bah! It's a hole, just as Pompanet says."

Torin leaned across the table and laid a heavy hand humanely on my shoulder.

"Take my advice," said he, "don't give up that snug farm of yours here for a lost hole like Pont du Sable."

"But the sea-shooting is open there three hundred and sixty-five days in the year," I protested, with enthusiasm. "I'm tired of tramping my legs off here for a few partridges a season. Besides, what I've been looking for I've found — a fine old abandoned house with a splendid old courtyard and a wild garden. I had the good luck to climb over a wall and discover it."

"I know the place you mean," interrupted the mayor. "It was a post-tavern in the old days before the railroad ran there."

"And later belonged to the estate of the Marquis de Lys," I added proudly. "Now it belongs to me."

"What! You've bought it!" exclaimed Torin, half closing his veal-like eyes.

"Yes," I confessed, "signed, sealed, and paid for."

"And what the devil do you intend to do with that old stone pile now that you've got it?" sneered Jaclin. "Ah! You artists are queer fellows!"

"Live in it, messieurs," I returned as happily as I could, as I dropped six sous for my glass into Madame Fontaine's open palm, and took my leave, for under the torrent of their protest I was beginning to feel I had been a fool to be carried away by my love of a gun and the picturesque.

The marsh at Pont du Sable was an old friend of mine. So were the desert beach beyond the dunes, and the lost fishing-village — "no longer than your arm." I had tramped in wind and rain and the good sunlight over that great desert of pasty black clay at low tide. I had lain at high tide in a sand-pit at the edge of the open sea beyond the dunes, waiting for chance shots at curlew and snipe. I had known the bay at the first glimmer of dawn with a flight of silver plovers wheeling for a rush over my decoys Dawn — the lazy, sparkling noon and the golden hours before the crisp, still twilight warned me it was high time to start back to Bar la Rose fourteen kilometres distant. All these had become enchanting memories.

Thus going to Pont du Sable for a day's shooting became a weekly delight, then a biweekly fascination, then an incorrigible triweekly habit.

There was no alternative left me now but to live there. The charm of that wild bay and its lost village had gotten under my skin. And thus it happened that I deserted my farm and friends at Bar la Rose, and with my goods and chattels boarded the toy train one spring morning, bound for my abandoned house, away from sufficient-unto-itself Bar la Rose and its pig-headed inhabitants, the butcher, the blacksmith, and the mayor.

It is such a funny little train that runs to my new-found Paradise, rocking and puffing and grumbling along on its narrow-gauge track with its cars labelled like grown-up ones, first, second, and third class; and no two painted the same colour; and its noisy, squat engine like the real ones in the toy-stores, that wind up with a key and go rushing off frantically in tangents. No wonder the train to my lost village is called "*Le petit déraillard*" — "The little get-off-the-track." And so I say, it might all have come packed in excelsior in a neat box, complete, with instructions, for the sum of four francs

sixty-five centimes, had it not been otherwise
destined to run twice daily, rain or shine, to
Pont du Sable, and beyond.

Poor little train! It is never on time, but
it does its best. It is at least far more prompt
than its passengers, for most of them come
running after it out of breath.

"Hurry up, mademoiselle!" cries the engineer to a rosy-cheeked girl in sabots, rushing with a market-basket under one arm and a
live goose under the other. "Eh, my little
lady, you should have gotten out of bed earlier!"
laughs the conductor as he pulls her aboard.

"Toot! Toot!" And off goes the little
get-off-the-track again, rocking and rumbling
along past desert stretches of sand dunes screening the blue sea; past modern villas, isolated
horrors in brick, pink, and baby blue, carefully
planted away from the trees. Then suddenly
the desert is left behind! Past the greenest of
fields now, dotted with sleek, grazing cattle;
past groves of pine; past snug Norman farms
with low-thatched roofs half-smothered in yellow
roses. Again the dunes, as the toy train swings

nearer the sea.   They are no longer desert wastes
of sand and wire-grass, but covered now with a
riot of growing things, running in one rich con-
gested sweep of orchards, pastures, feathery
woodlands and matted hedges down to the very
edge of the blue sea.

A sudden turn, and the toy train creeps out
of a grove of pines to the open bay.   It is high
tide.   A flight of plover, startled by the engine,
go wheeling away in a silver streak to a spit of
sand running out from the marsh.   A puff of
smoke from the sand-spit, and the band leaves
two of its members to a gentleman in new
leather leggings; then, whistling over the calam-
ity that has befallen them, they wheel again and
strike for the open sea and safety.

Far across the expanse of rippling turquoise
water stands a white lighthouse that at dusk
is set with a yellow diamond.   Snug at the
lower end of the bay, a long mile from where
the plovers rise, lies the lost village.   Now the
toy train is crawling through its crooked single
street, the engine-bell ringing furiously that stray
dogs and children, and a panicky flock of sheep

may have time to get out of the way. The sheep are in charge of a rough little dog with a cast in one eye and a slim, barelegged girl who apologizes a dozen times to monsieur the engineer between her cries to her flock.

"They are not very well brought up, my little one — those sacred mutton of yours," remarks the engineer as he comes to a dead stop, jumps out of his cab, and helps straighten out the tangle.

"Ah, monsieur!" sighs the girl in despair. "What will you have? It is the little black one that is always to blame!"

The busy dog crowds them steadily into line. He seems to be everywhere at once, darting from right to left, now rounding up a stubborn ewe and her first-born, now cornering the black one.

"Toot! Toot!" And the little get-off-the-track goes rumbling on through the village, past the homes of the fishermen — a straggling line of low stone houses with quaint gabled roofs, and still quainter chimneys, and old doorways giving glimpses of dark interiors and dirt floors. Past the modest houses of the mayor, the baker,

the butcher and Monsieur le Curé; then through
the small public square, in which nothing ever
happens, and up to a box of a station.

"Pont du Sable!" cries the conductor, with
as much importance as if he had announced
Paris.

I have arrived.

There was no doubt about my new-found
home being abandoned! The low stone wall
that tempered the wind from courtyard and
garden was green with lichens. The wide stone
gateway, with its oaken doors barred within by
massive cross-hooks that could have withstood
a siege; the courtyard, flanked by the house and
its rambling appendages that contained within
their cavernous interiors the cider-press and
cellars; the stable with its long stone manger,
and next it the carved wooden bunk for the
groom of two centuries ago; the stone pig-sty;
the tile-roofed sheds — all had about them the
charm of dignified decay.

But the "château" itself!

Generations of spiders had veiled every nook

and corner within, and the nooks and corners
were many. These cobwebs hung in ghostly
festoons from the low-beamed ceiling of the
living room, opening out upon the wild garden.
They continued up the narrow stone stairway
leading to the old-fashioned stone-paved bedrooms; they had been spun in a labyrinth all
over the generous, spooky, old stone-paved attic,
whose single eye of a window looked out over
the quaint gables and undulating tiled roofs of
adjoining attics, whose dark interiors were still
pungent with the tons of apples they had once
sheltered. Beyond my rambling roofs were
rich orchards and noble trees and two cool
winding lanes running up to the green country
beyond.

Ten days of strenuous settling passed, at
the end of which my abandoned house was
resuscitated, as it were. Without Suzette, my
little maid-of-all-work, it would have been
impossible. I may say we attacked this seemingly superhuman task together — and Suzette
is so human. She has that frantic courage of
youth, and a smile that is irresistible.

"To-morrow monsieur shall see," she said. "My kitchen is clean — that is something, eh? And the beds are up, and the armoires, and nearly all of monsieur's old studio furniture in place. *Eh, ben!* To-morrow night shall see most of the sketches hung and the rugs beaten — that is again something, eh? Then there will be only the brass and the andirons and the guns to clean."

Ten days of strenuous attack, sometimes in the rain, and when I hammer my fingers in the rain I swear horribly; the average French saw, too, would have placed Job in a sanitarium. Suzette's cheery smile is a delight, and how her sturdy, dimpled arms can scrub, and dust, and cook, and clean. When she is working at full steam she invariably sings; but when her soufflé does not soufflé she bursts into tears — this good little peasant maid-of-all-work!

And so the abandoned house by the marsh was settled. Now there is charm, and crackling fires o' nights within, and sunny breakfasts in the garden without — a garden that grew to be

gay with flowers, and is still in any wind, thanks
to my friend the lichen-stained wall over which
clamber vines and all manner of growing things;
and sometimes my kitten with her snow-white
breast, whose innocent green eyes narrow to
slits as she watches for hours two little birds
that are trying to bring up a small family in the
vines.   I have told her plainly if she even touches
them I will boil her in oil.   "Do you hear,
Miquette?" and she turns away and licks her
pink paw as if she had not heard — you essence
of selfishness that I love!

Shall I tell you who is coming to dine to-night,
Green-eyes?   Our neighbours! Madame Alice
de Bréville who spoils you, and the Marquis de
Clamard who does not like pussy-cats, but is
too well-bred to tell you so, and the marquise
who flatters you, and Blondel!   Don't struggle
— you cannot get away, I've got you tight.
You are not going to have your way all the time.
Look at me!   Claws in and your ears up!
There!   And Tanrade, that big, whole-souled
musician, with his snug old house and his two
big dogs, either one of which would make mince-

meat of you should you have the misfortune to mistake his garden for your own. Madame de Bréville — do you hear? — who has but to half close her eyes to make Tanrade forget his name. He loves her madly, you see, pussy-kit!

Ah, yes! The lost village! In which the hours are never dull. Lost village! With these Parisian neighbours, whose day of discovery antedated mine by several years. Lost village! In which there are jolly fishermen and fisher-girls as pretty as some gipsies — slim and fear-less, a genial old mayor, an optimistic black-smith, and a butcher who is a seigneur; gentle old women in white caps, blue-eyed children, kind dogs, fresh air, and *life!*

There is a mysterious fascination about that half-hour before the first glimmer of dawn. The leaves, this September morning, are shiver-ing in the dusk of my garden; the house is as silent as my sleeping cat save for the resonant tick-tock, tick-tock, of the tall Norman clock in the kitchen, to which I tiptoe down and breakfast by candle-light.

You should see the Essence of Selfishness
then as she purrs around a simmering sauce-
pan of milk destined for my coffee, and inspects
the toast and jam, and sniffs at my breech-loader,
well greased with neatsfoot-oil, and now the
ghostly light in the courtyard tells me to hurry
out on the bay.

Low tide. Far out on the desert of black
clay a colony of gulls have spent the night.
Their quarrelsome jargon reaches me as I
cautiously raise my head over the dunes, for
often a band of plover is feeding at dawn out
on the mud, close enough for a shot.   Nothing
in view save the gulls, those gossiping concierges
of the bay, who rise like a squall of snow as I
make a clean breast of my presence, and start
across the soggy, slippery mud toward the marsh
running out to the open sea.   A curlew, motion-
less on his long legs, calls cheerfully from the
point of sand: "Curli — Curli!"   Strong, cheer-
ful old bird.   The rifts of white mist are lifting
from the bay, thinned into rose vapour now, as
the sun creeps above the green hillsides.

Swish! Three silver plovers flash back of

me — a clean miss. If we never missed we should never love a gun. It is time now to stalk the bottoms of the narrow, winding causeways that drain the bay. Their beds at low tide are full of dead mussels, dormant clams, and awkward sputtering crabs; the old ones sidling away from you with threatening claws wide open for combat; the young ones standing their ground bravely, in ignorance.

Swish again! But this time I manage to kill them both — two fat golden plovers. The Essence of Selfishness shall have her fill at noon, and the pupils of her green eyes will contract in ecstasy as she crunches and gnaws.

Now all the bay is alive. Moreover, the sea is sweeping in, filling the bay like a bath-tub, obliterating the causeways under millions of dancing ripples of turquoise. Soon my decoys are out, and I am sunk in a sand-pit at the edge of the sea. The wind holds strong from the northeast, and I am kept busy until my gun-barrels are too hot to be pleasant. All these things happen between dawn and a late breakfast in my garden.

Suzette sang all day. It is always so with
Suzette upon the days when the abandoned
house is giving a dinner. The truth is, Suzette
loves to cook; her pride and her happiness
increase as the hour appointed for my guests to
arrive approaches. With Suzette it is a delightful event.

The cracked jingle-bell over my stone gateway had jingled incessantly since early morning,
summoning this good little Norman maid-of-
all-work to slip her trim feet into her sabots
and rush across the court to open the small
door piercing my wall beside the big gates.
Twice for beggars, once for the grocer's boy,
three times for the baker — who had, after all,
forgotten the *brioche;* again for the baker's
boy, who invariably forgets if he thinks there is
another chance in his forgetting, of paying a
forgotten compliment to Suzette. I heard his
mother scolding him yesterday. His bread,
which he kneads and bakes himself before
dawn, is losing its lightness. There is little
harmony between rising yeast and a failing
heart. Again the bell jingles; this time it is

the Mère Marianne, with a basket of quivering, iridescent mackerel just in from the night's fishing.

Mère Marianne, who once was a village belle, is now thirty-three years of age, strong as a man, fair-haired, hatless, bronzed by the sun, salt-tanned, blue-eyed, a good mother to seven fair-haired, blue-eyed children; yet a hard, amiable drinker in her leisure hours after a good catch.

"*Bonjour*, my all beautiful!" she greets Suzette as the door opens.

"*Bonjour*, madame!" returns Suzette, her cheeks flushed from her kitchen fire.

The word "madame" seems out of place, for Mère Marianne wears her man's short tarpaulin coat cinched about her waist with a thin tarred rope. Her sinewy legs, bare to the knees, are tightly incased in a pair of sea-soaked trousers.

"So monsieur is having his friends to dinner," she rattles on garrulously, swinging her basket to the ground and kneeling before it. "I heard it as I came up the road from Blancheville's

girl, who had it from the Mère Taurville. *Eh
ben!* What do you think of these?" she adds
in the same breath, as she turns up two hands-
ful of live mackerel. "Six sous apiece to you,
my pretty one. You see I came to you first;
I'm giving them to you as cheap as if you were
my own daughter."

"Come, be quick," returns Suzette. "I have
my lobster to boil and my roast to get ready;
four sous if you like, but not a sou more."

"Four sous! *Bon Dieu!* I would rather eat
them myself. They only lack speech to tell you
themselves how fresh they are. Look at them!"

"Four sous," insists Suzette. "Do you
think monsieur is rich enough to buy the
république."

"*Allez!* Then, take them at four sous."
And Mère Marianne laughs, slips the money
into her trousers pocket, and goes off to another
bargain in the village, where, if she gets two
sous for her mackerel she will be lucky.

At six Suzette lifts the Burgundy tenderly
from its resting-place in a closet beneath the
winding stone stairs — a stone closet, low,

,sinister, and dark, that suggests the solitary dungeons of feudal times. Three cobwebbed bottles of Burgundy are now carefully ranged before the crackling blaze in the living room. At six-thirty Suzette lays the generous dark-oak table in lace and silver, thin glasses, red-shaded candles, and roses — plenty of roses from the garden.

Her kitchen by this time is no longer open to visitors. It has become a sacred place, teeming with responsibility — a laboratory of resplendent shining copper sauce-pans, pots and casseroles, in which good things steam and stew and bubble under lids of burnished gold, which, when lifted, give one a rousing appetite.

I knew Tanrade's ring — vigorous and hearty, like himself. You would never guess this sturdy, broad-shouldered man has created delicious music — fairy ballets, pantomimes, and oper-ettas. All Paris has applauded him for years, and his country has rewarded him with a narrow red ribbon. Rough-bearded, bronzed like a sailor, his brown eyes gleam with kindness and intelligence. The more I know this modest

great man the more I like him, and I have
known him in all kinds of wind and weather,
for Tanrade is an indefatigable hunter.   He and
I have spent nights together in his duck-blind
— a submerged hut, a murderous deceit sunk
far out on the marsh — cold nights; soft moonlight nights — the marsh a mystic fairy-land;
black nights — mean nights of thrashing rain.
Nights that paled to dawn with no luck to bring
back to Suzette's larder.   Sunny mornings after
lucky nights, when Tanrade and I would thaw out
over our coffee in the garden among the roses.

Tanrade had arrived early, a habit with this
genial gourmand when the abandoned house
is giving a dinner, for he likes to supervise the
final touches.   He was looking critically over
the three cobwebbed bottles of his favourite
Burgundy now warming before my fire, and
having tenderly lifted the last bottle in the row
to a place which he considered a safer temperature, he straightened and squared his
broad shoulders to the blaze.

"I'll send you half a dozen more bottles
to-morrow," he said.

"No, you won't, my old one," I protested, but he raised his hand and smiled.

"The better the wine the merrier shall be the giver. Eighteen bottles left! *Eh bien!* It was a lucky day when that monastery was forced to disband," he chuckled, alluding to the recent separation of the church from the state. "*Vive la République!*" He crossed the room to the sideboard and, having assured himself the Camembert was of the right age, went singing into Suzette's kitchen to glance at the salad.

"Bravo, my little one, for your romaine!" I heard him exclaim.

Then a moment's silence ensued, while he tasted the dressing. "*Sacristi!* My child, do you think we are rabbits. *Hélas!* Not a bit of astragon in your seasoning! A thousand thunders! A salad is not a salad without astragon. Come, be quick, the lantern! I know where the bed is in the garden."

"Ah, monsieur Tanrade! To think I should have forgotten it!" sighed the little maid. "If monsieur will only let me hold the lantern for him!"

"There, there! Never mind! See, you are forgiven. Attend to your lobster. Quick, your soup is boiling over!" And he went out into the garden in search of the seasoning.

Suzette adores him — who does not in the lost village? He had rewarded her with a two-franc piece and forgiven her with a kiss.

I had hardly time to open the big gates without and light the candles within under their red shades glowing over the mass of roses still wet from the garden, before I heard the devilish wail of a siren beyond the wall; then a sudden flash of white light from two search-lights illumined the courtyard, and with a wrenching growl Madame Alice de Breville's automobile whined up to my door. The next instant the tip of a little patent-leather slipper, followed by the trimmest of silken ankles framed in a frou-frou of creamy lace, felt for the steel step of the limousine. At the same moment a small white-gloved hand was outstretched to mine for support.

"*Bonsoir*, dear friend," she greeted me in her delicious voice. "You see how punctual

I am.   *L'heure militaire* — like you Americans."
And she laughed outright, disclosing two exquisite rows of pearls, her soft, dark eyes half
closing mischievously as she entered my door —
eyes as black as her hair, which she wore in a
bandeau.   The tonneau growled to its impro-
vised garage under the wood-shed.

She was standing now in the hall at the foot
of the narrow stone stairs, and as I slipped the
long opera-cloak of dove-gray from her shoulders
as white as ivory, she glided out of it, and into
the living room — a room which serves as gun
room, dining room and salon.

"Stand where you are," I said, as madame
approached the fire.   "What a portrait!"

She stopped, the dancing light from the flames
playing over her lithe, exquisite figure, moulded
in a gown of scintillating scales of black jet.
Then, seeing I had finished my mental note of
line and composition, she half turned her pretty
head and caught sight of the ruby, cobwebbed
row of old Burgundy.

"Ah!   Tanrade's Burgundy!" she exclaimed
with a little cry of delight.

"How did you guess?"

"Guess! One does not have to guess when one sees as good Burgundy as that. You see I know it." She stretched forth her firm white arms to the blaze.

"Where is he, that good-for-nothing fellow?" she asked.

"In the garden after some astragon for the salad."

She tripped to the half-open door leading to the tangled maze of paths.

"Tanrade! Tanrade! *Bonsoir, ami!*" she called.

"*Bonsoir*, Madame Punctual," echoed his great voice from the end of the garden, and again he broke forth in song as he came hurrying back to the house with his lantern and his bunch of seasoning. Following at his heels trotted the Essence of Selfishness.

"Oh, you beauty!" cried Alice. She nodded mischievously to Tanrade, who rushed to the piano, and before the Essence of Selfishness had time to elude her she was picked up bodily, held by her fore paws and forced to dance upon her hind legs, her sleek head turned aside in hate, her velvety ears flattened to her skull.

"Dance! Dance!" laughed Alice. "One — two, one — two! *Voilà!*" The next instant Miquette was caught up and hugged to a soft neck encircled with jewels. "There, go! Do what you like, Mademoiselle Independent!"

And as Miquette regained her liberty upon her four paws, the Marquis and Marquise de Clamard announced their arrival by tapping on the window, so that for the moment the cozy room was deserted save by Miquette, who profited during the interval by stealing a whole sardine from the hors-d'œuvres.

Another good fellow is the marquis — tall, with the air of a diplomat, the simplicity of a child, and the manners of a prince. Another good friend, too, is the marquise. They had come on foot, these near-by neighbours, with their lantern. Was there ever such a marquise? This once famous actress, who interpreted the comedies of Molière. Was there ever a more charming grandmother? Ah! You do not look it even now with your gray hair, for you are ever

young and witty and gracious. She clapped
her hands as she peered across the dinner-table
to the row before the chimney.

"My Burgundy, I see!" she exclaimed, to
my surprise; Tanrade was gazing intently at a
sketch. "Oh, you shall see," added the marquise seriously. "You are not the only one,
my friend, the gods have blessed. Did you not
send me a dozen bottles this morning, Monsieur
Tanrade? Come, confess!"

He turned and shrugged his shoulders.

"Impossible! I cannot remember. I am so
absent-minded, madame," and he bent and
kissed her hand.

"Where's Blondel?" cried Clamard, as he
extracted a thin cigarette-case from his waistcoat.

"He'll be here presently," I explained.

"It's a long drive for him," added the marquise, a ring of sympathy in her voice. "Poor
boy, he is working so hard now that he is editor
of *La Revue Normande*. Ah, those wretched
politics!"

"He doesn't mind it," broke in Tanrade,
"he has a skin like a bear — driving night and

day all over the country as he does. What
energy, *mon Dieu!*"

"Oh!" cried Madame de Bréville, "Blondel
shall sing for us 'L'Histoire de Madame X.'
You shall cry with laughter."

"And 'Le Brigadier de Tours,'" added Tanrade.

The sound of hoofs and the rattle of a dog-
cart beyond the wall sent us hurrying to the
courtyard.

"*Eh, voilà!*" shouted Tanrade. "There he
is, that good Blondel!"

"Suzette!" I cried as I passed the kitchen.
"The vermouth!"

"*Bien*, monsieur."

"Eh, Blondel, there is nothing to eat, you
late vagabond!"

A black mare steaming from her hot pace of
twelve miles, drawing a red-wheeled dog-cart,
entered the courtyard.

"A thousand pardons," came a voice out
of a bearskin coat, "my editorial had to go to
press early, or I should have been here half an
hour ago."

Then such a greeting and a general rush to unharness the tired mare, the marquis tugging at one trace and I at the other, while Tanrade backed the cart under the shed next to the cider-press, Alice de Bréville and the marquise holding the mare's head. All this, despite the pleadings of Blondel, who has a horror of giving trouble — the only man servant to the abandoned house being Pierre, who was occupied at that hour in patrolling the coast in the employ of the French République, looking out for possible smugglers, and in whose spare hours served me as gardener. And so the mare was led into the stable with its stone manger, where every one helped with halter, blanket, a warm bed, and a good supper; Alice de Bréville holding the lantern while the marquise bound on the mare's blanket with a girdle of straw.

"Monsieur, dinner is served," announced Suzette gently as she entered the stable.

"*Vive* Suzette!" shouted the company. "*Allons manger, mes enfants!*"

They found their places at the table by themselves. In the abandoned house there is neither

host nor formality, but in their stead comrade-
ship, understanding, and good cheer.

Blondel is delightful. You can always count
on him for the current events with the soup, the
latest scandal with the roast, and a song of his
own making with the cheese. What more can
one ask? It all rolls from him as easily as the
ink from his clever pen; it is as natural with him
as his smile or the merriment in his eyes.

During the entire dinner the Essence of Selfishness was busy visiting from one friendly lap
to another, frequently crossing the table to do so,
and as she refuses to dine from a saucer, though it
be of the finest porcelain of Rouen, she was fed
piecemeal. It was easily seen Tanrade was envi-
ous of this charity from one shapely little hand.

What a contrast are these dinners in the lost
village to some I have known elsewhere! What
refreshing vivacity! How genuine and merry
they are from the arrival of the first guest to the
going of the last! When at last the coffee and
liqueurs were reached and six thin spirals of
blue smoke were curling lazily up among the
rafters of the low ceiling, the small upright piano

talked under Tanrade's vibrant touch.   He sang
heartily whatever came into his head; now a
quaint peasant song, again the latest success of
the café concert.

Alice de Bréville, stretched out in the long
chair before the fire, was listening intently.

And so with song and story the hands of the
tall clock slipped by the hours.   It was midnight
before we knew it.   Again Tanrade played —
this time it was the second act of his new operetta.
When he had finished he took his seat beside the
woman in the long chair.

"Bravo!" she murmured in his ear.   Then
she listened as he talked to her earnestly.

"Good!" I overheard her say to him with conviction, her eyes gleaming.   "And you are satisfied at last with the second act?"

"Yes, after a month's struggle with it."

"Ah, I am so glad — so glad!" she sighed,
and pressed his hand.

"I must go to Paris next week for the rehearsals."

"For long?" she asked.

He shrugged his shoulders helplessly.   "For

weeks, perhaps. Come," he said, "let us go out to the wall — the moon is up. The marsh is so beautiful in the moonlight."

She rose, slipped on the dove-gray cloak he brought her, and together they disappeared in the courtyard. The marquise raised her eyes to mine and smiled.

"*Bonne promenade*, dear children," she called after them, but they did not hear.

An hour later Alice de Bréville was speeding back to her château; Blondel and his mare were also clattering homeward, for he had still an article to finish before daylight. I had just bid the marquis and the marquise good night when Tanrade, who was about to follow, suddenly turned and called me aside in the shadow of the gateway. What he said to me made my heart leap. His eyes were shining with a strange light; his hands, gripping me by both shoulders, trembled.

"It is true," he repeated. "Don't tell me I am dreaming, old friend. Yes, it is true. Alice — yes, it is Alice. Come, a glass of wine! I feel faint — and happy!"

We went back to the dying fire, and I believe he heard all my congratulations, though I am not sure. He seemed in a dream.

When he had gone Suzette lighted my candle.

"Suzette," I said, "your dinner was a success."

"Ah, but I am content, monsieur. *Mon Dieu*, but I do love to cook!"

"Come, Miquette! It's past your bedtime, you adorable egoist."

"*Bonsoir*, Suzette."

"*Bonsoir*, monsieur."

Village of Vagabonds! In which the hours are never dull! Lost village by the Normand sea! In which lies a paradise of good-fellowship, romance, love, and sound red wine!

CHAPTER TWO

MONSIEUR LE CURÉ

THE sun had just risen, and the bell of the little stone church chattered and jangled, flinging its impatient call over the sleeping village of Pont du Sable. In the clear morning air its voice could be heard to the tops of the green hills, and across the wide salt marsh that stretched its feathery fingers to the open sea.

A lone, wrinkled fisherman, rolling lazily on the mighty heave of the incoming tide, turned his head landward.

"*Sapristi!*" he grinned, as he slipped a slimy thumb from the meshes of a mackerel-net and crossed himself. "She has a hoarse throat, that little one."

Far up the hillside a mile back of the church-
yard, a barelegged girl driving a cow stopped to
listen, her hood pushed back, her brown hands
crossed upon her breast.

Lower down, skirting the velvet edge of the
marsh, filmy rifts of mist broke into shreds or
blended with the spirals of blue smoke mounting
skyward from freshly kindled fires.

Pont du Sable was awake for the day.

It is the most unimportant of little villages,
yet it is four centuries old, and of stone. It
seems to have shrivelled by its great age, like its
oldest inhabitants. One-half of its two score
of fishermen's houses lie crouched to the rambling edge of its single street; the other half might
have been dropped at random, like stones from
the pocket of some hurrying giant. Some of
these, including the house of the ruddy little
mayor and the polite, florid grocer, lie spilled
along the edge of the marsh.

As for Monsieur le Curé, he was at this very
moment in the small stone church saying mass
to five fishermen, two devout housewives, a little
child, an old woman in a white cap, and myself.

Being in my shooting-boots, I had tiptoed into a
back seat behind two of the fishermen, and sat
in silence watching Monsieur le Curé's gaunt
figure and listening to his deep, well-modulated,
resonant voice.

What I saw was a man uncommonly tall and
well built, dressed in a rusty black soutane that
reached in straight lines from beneath his chin
to his feet, which were encased in low calf shoes
with steel buckles.   I noticed, too, that his face
was angular and humorous; his eyes keen and
merry by turns; his hair of the colourless brown
one sees among fisherfolk whose lives are spent
in the sun and rain.   I saw, too, that he was
impecunious, for the front edges of his cassock
were frayed and three buttons missing, not to be
wondered at, I said to myself, as I remembered
that the stone church, like the village it com-
forted, had always been poor.

Now and then during the mass I saw the curé
glance at the small leaded window above him
as if making a mental note of the swaying tree-
tops without in the graveyard.   Then his keen
gray eyes again reverted to the page he knew

by heart. The look evidently carried some sig-
nificance, for the gray-haired old sea-dog in front
of me cocked his blue eye to his partner — they
were both in from a rough night's fishing —
and muttered:

"It will be a short mass."

"*Ben sûr,*" whispered back the other from
behind his leathery hand. "The wind's from the
northeast. It will blow a gale before sundown."
And he nodded toward the swaying tree-tops.

With this, the one with the blue eyes straightened back in the wooden pew and folded his
short, knotty arms in attention; the muscles of
his broad shoulders showing under his thick
seaman's jersey, the collar encircling his corded,
stocky neck deep-seamed by a thousand winds
and seas. The gestures of these two old crafts-
men of the sea, who had worked so long together,
were strangely similar. When they knelt I
could see the straw sticking from the heels of
their four wooden sabots and the rolled-up bottoms of their patched sail-cloth trousers.

As the mass ended the old woman in the white
cap coughed gently, the curé closed his book,

stepped from the chancel, patted the child's head in passing, strode rapidly to the sacristy, and closed the door behind him.

I followed the handful of worshippers out into the sunlight and down the hill. As I passed the two old fishermen I heard the one with the blue eyes say to his mate with the leathery hand:

"*Allons, viens t'en!* What if we went to the café after that dog's night of a sea?"

"I don't say no," returned his partner; then he winked at me and pointed to the sky.

"I know," I said. "It's what I've been waiting for."

I kept on down the crooked hill to the public square where nothing ever happens save the arrival of the toy train and the yearly fête, and deciding the two old salts were right after their "dog's night" (and it had blown a gale), wheeled to the left and followed them to the tiniest of cafés kept by stout, cheery Madame Vinet. It has a box of a kitchen through which you pass into a little square room with just space enough for four tables; or you may go through the kitchen into a snug garden gay

in geraniums and find a sheltered table beneath
a rickety arbour.

"Ah, *mais*, it was bad enough!" grinned the
one with the leathery hand as he drained his
thimbleful of applejack and, Norman-like, tossed
the last drop on the floor of the snug room.

"Bad enough!   It was a sea, I tell you, monsieur, like none since the night the wreck
of *La Belle Marie* came ashore," chimed in the
one with the blue eye, as he placed his elbows on
the clean marbletop table and made room for my
chair.   "*Mon Dieu!*   You should have seen the
ducks south of the Wolf.   Aye, 'twas a sight for
an empty stomach."

The one with the leathery hand nodded his
confirmation sleepily.

"*Hélas!*" continued the one with the blue eye.
"If monsieur could only have been with us!"
As he spoke he lifted his shaggy eyebrows in the
direction of the church and laughed softly.
"He's happy with his northeast wind; I knew
'twould be a short mass."

"A good catch?" I ventured, looking toward
him as Madame Vinet brought my glass.

"Eight thousand mackerel, monsieur. We should have had ten thousand had not the wind shifted."

"*Ben sûr!*" grumbled the one with the leathery hand.

At this Madame Vinet planted her fists on her ample hips. "*Hélas!* There's the Mère Coraline's girl to be married Thursday," she sighed, "and Planchette's baby to be christened Tuesday, and the wind in the northeast, *mon Dieu!*" And she went back to her spotless kitchen for a sou's worth of black coffee for a little girl who had just entered.

Big, strong, hearty Madame Vinet! She has the frankness of a man and the tenderness of a mother. There is something of her youth still left at forty-six; not her figure — that is rotund simplicity itself — but in the clearness of her brown eyes and the finely cut profile before it reaches her double chin, and the dimples in her hands, well shaped even to-day.

And so the little girl who had come in for the sou's worth of coffee received an honest measure, smoking hot out of a dipper and into the bottle she had brought. In payment Madame Vinet kissed the child, and added a lump of sugar to the bargain. From where I sat I could see the tears start in the good woman's eyes. The next moment she came back to us laughing to disguise them.

"Ah, you good soul!" I thought to myself. "Always in a good humour; always pleasant. There you go again — this time it was the wife of a poor fisherman who could not pay. How many a poor devil of a half-frozen sailor you have warmed, you whose heart is so big and whose gains are so small!"

I rose at length, bade the two old salts good morning, and with a blessing of good luck, recovered my gun from the kitchen cupboard, where I had reverently left it during mass, and went on my way to shoot. I, too, was anxious to make the most of the northeast wind.

There being no street in the lost village save the main thoroughfare, one finds only alleys flanked by rambling walls. One of these runs up to Tanrade's house; another finds its zig-

zag way to the back gate of the marquis, who,
being a royalist, insists upon telling you so, for
the keystone of his gate is emblazoned with a
bas-relief of two carved eagles guarding the family crest. Still another leads unexpectedly to the
silent garden of Monsieur le Curé. It is a pro-
tecting little by-way whose walls tell no tales.
How many a suffering heart seeking human sympathy and advice has the strong figure in the
soutane sent home with fresh courage by way of
this back lane. Indeed it would be a lost village without him. He is barely over forty years
old, and yet no curé was ever given a poorer
parish, for Pont du Sable has been bankrupt
for generations. Since a fortnight — so I am
told — Monsieur le Curé has had no *bonne*.
The reason is that no good Suzette can be found
to replace the one whom he married to a young
farmer from Bonville. The result is the good
curé dines many times a week with the marquis,
where he is so entertaining and so altogether
delightful and welcome a guest that the marquise tells me she feels ten years younger after
he has gone.

"Poor man," she confided to me the other
day, "what will you have? He has no *bonne*,
and he detests cooking. Yesterday he lunched
at the château with Alice de Bréville; to-morrow
he will be cheering up two old maiden aunts who
live a league from Bar la Rose. Is it not sad?"
And she laughed merrily.

"Monsieur le Curé has no *bonne!*" *Parbleu!*
It has become a household phrase in Pont du
Sable. It is so difficult to get a servant here;
the girls are all fishing. As for Tanrade's maid-
of-all-work, like the noiseless butler of the marquis and the *femme de chambre* of Alice de
Bréville, they are all from Paris; and yet I'll
wager that no larder in the village is better
stocked than Monsieur le Curé's, for every house-
wife vies with her neighbour in ready-cooked
donations since the young man from Bonville was
accepted.

But these good people do not forget. They
remember the day when the farm of Père Marin
burned; they recall the figure in the black soutane
stumbling on through flame and smoke carrying
an unconscious little girl in his strong arms to

safety. Four times he went back where no man dared go — and each time came out with a life.

Again, but for his indomitable grit, a half-drowned father and daughter, clinging to a capsized fishing-smack in a winter sea, would not be alive — there are even fisherfolk who cannot swim. Monsieur le Curé saw this at a glance, alone he fought his way in the freezing surf out to the girl and the man. He brought them in and they lived.

But there is a short cut to the marsh if you do but know it — one that has served me before. You can easily find it, for you have but to follow your nose along the wall of Madame Vinet's café, creep past the modest rose-garden of the mayor, zigzag for a hundred paces or more among crumbling walls, and before you know it you are out on the marsh.

The one with the blue eye was right.

The wind *was* from the northeast in earnest, and the tide racing in. Half a mile outward a dozen long puntlike scows, loaded to their brims

with sand, were being borne on the swirling current up the river's channel, each guided at the
stern by a ragged dot of a figure straining at an
oar.

As I struck out across the desolate waste of
mud, bound for the point of dry marsh, the figure steering the last scow, as he passed, waved
a warning to me. With the incoming sweep of
tide the sunlight faded, the bay became noisy
with the cries of sea-fowl, and the lighthouse
beyond the river's channel stood out against the
ominous green sky like a stick of school-chalk.

I jerked my cap tighter over my ears, and
lowering my head to the wind kept on. I had
barely time to make the marsh. Over the black
desolate waste of clay-mud the sea was spreading its hands — long, dangerous hands, with
fingers that every moment shot out longer and
nearer my tracks. The wind blew in howling
gusts now, straight in from the open sea. Days
like these the ducks have no alternative but the
bay. Only a black diver can stand the strain
outside. Tough old pirates these — diving to
keep warm.

I kept on, foolish as it was. A flight of becas-
sines were whirled past me, twittering in a panic
as they fought their way out of sudden squalls.
I turned to look back. Already my sunken
tracks were obliterated under a glaze of water,
but I felt I was safe, for I had gained harder
ground. It was a relief to slide to the bottom
of one of the labyrinth of causeways that drain
the marsh, and plunge on sheltered from the
wind.

Presently I heard ducks quacking ahead. I
raised my head cautiously to the level of the wire-
grass. A hundred rods beyond, nine black
ducks were grouped near the edge of a circular
pool; behind them, from where I stood, there
rose from the level waste a humplike mound.
I could no longer proceed along the bottom of
the causeway, as it was being rapidly filled to
within an inch below my boot-tops. The hump
was my only salvation, so I crawled to the bank
and started to stalk the nine black ducks.

It was difficult to keep on my feet on the slimy
mud-bank, for the wind, true to the fishermen's
prediction, was now blowing half a gale. Be-

sides, this portion of the marsh was strange
to me, as I had only seen it at a distance from
the lower end of the bay, where I generally shot.
I was within range of the ducks now, and had
raised my hammers — I still shoot a hammer-
gun — when a human voice rang out.   Then,
like some weird jack-in-the-box, there popped
out from the mound a straight, long-waisted
body in black waving its arms.

It was the curé!

"Stay where you are," he shouted.   "Treacherous ground!   I'll come and help you!"   Then
for a second he peered intently under his hand.
"Ah!   It is you, monsieur — the newcomer; I
might have guessed it."   He laughed, leaping
out and striding toward me.   "Ah, you Americans!   You do not mind the weather."

"*Bonjour*, Monsieur le Curé," I shouted
back in astonishment, trying to steady myself
across a narrow bridge of mud spanning the
causeway.

"Look out!" he cried.   "That mud you're
on is dangerous.   She's sinking!"

It was too late; my right foot barely made

another step before down I went, gun, shells, and all, up to my chin in ice-cold water. The next instant he had me by the collar of my leather coat in a grip of steel, and I was hauled out, dripping and draining, on the bank.

"I'm all right," I sputtered.

"Come inside *instantly*," he said.

"Inside? Inside where?" I asked.

He pointed to the hump.

"You must get your wet things off and into bed at once." This came as a command.

"Bed! Where? Whose bed?" Was he an Aladdin with a magic lamp, that could summon comfort in that desolation? "Monsieur," I choked, "I owe you a thousand apologies. I came near killing one of your nine decoys. I mistook them for wild mallards."

He laughed softly. "They are not mine," he explained. "They belong to the marquis; it is his gardener who pickets them out for me. I could not afford to keep them myself. They eat outrageously, those nine deceivers. They are well placed to-day; just the right distance." And he called the three nearest us by name,

for they were quacking loudly. "Be still, Fan-
nine! There, Pierrot! If your cord and swivel
does not work, my good drake, I'll fix it for you,
but don't make such a fuss; you'll have noise
enough to make later." And gripping me by the
arm, he pushed me firmly ahead of him to a small
open door in the mound. I peered into the
darkness within.

"Get in," said he. "It's small, but it's warm
and comfortable inside. After you, my friend,"
he added graciously, and we descended into a
narrow ditch, its end blocked by a small, safe-
like door leading into a subterranean hut, its
roof being the mound, shelving out to a semi-
circular, overhanging eyebrow skirting the edge
of the circular pool some ten yards back of the
line of live decoys.

"Ah!" exclaimed Monsieur le Curé, "you
should have seen the duck-blind I had three
years ago. This *gabion* of mine is smaller, but
it is in better line with the flights," he explained
as he opened the door. "Look out for the steps
— there are two."

I now stood shivering in the gloom of a box-

like, underground anteroom, provided with a
grated floor and a low ribbed ceiling; beyond
this, through another small door, was an adjoining compartment deeper than the one in which
we stood, and in the darkness I caught the out-
line of a cot-bed, a carved, high-backed, leather-
seated chair, and the blue glint of guns lying in
their racks.   The place was warm and smelled,
like the cabin of some fishing-sloop, of sea-salt
and tar.

It did not take me long to get out of my clothes.
When the last of them lay around my heels I
received a rubbing down with a coarse sailor's
shirt, that sent the blood back where it belonged.

"*Allons!* Into bed at once!" insisted the
curé. "You'll find those army blankets dry."

I felt my way in while he struck a match and
lighted a candle upon a narrow shelf strewn
with empty cartridges. The candle sputtered,
sunk to a blue flame, and flared up cheerfully,
while the curé poured me out a stiff glass of
brandy, and I lay warm in the blankets of the
Armée Française, and gazed about me at my
strange quarters.

Back of my pillow was, tightly closed, in three sections, a narrow firing-slit. Beside the bed the candle's glow played over the carved back of the leather-seated chair. Above the closed slit ran a shelf, and ranged upon it were some fifty cartridges and an old-fashioned fat opera-glass. This, then, was Monsieur le Curé's duck-blind, or rather, in French, his *gabion*.

The live decoys began quacking nervously. The curé, about to speak, tip-toed over to the firing-slit and let down cautiously one of its compartments.

"A flight of plovers passing over us," he remarked. "Yes, there they go. If the wind will only hold you shall see — there will be ducks in," his gray eyes beaming at the thought.

Then he drew the chair away from the firing-slit and seated himself, facing me.

"If you knew," he began, "how much it means to me to talk to one of the outside world — your country — America! You must tell me much about it. I have always longed to see it, but ——"
He shrugged his shoulders helplessly. "Are you warm?" he asked.

"Warm?" I laughed. "I never felt better in my life." And I thanked him again for his kindness to a stranger in distress. "A stranger in luck," I added.

"I saw you at mass this morning," he returned bending over, his hands on his knees. "But you are not a Catholic, my friend? You are always welcome to my church, however, remember that."

"Thank you," I said. "I like your little church, and — I like you, Monsieur le Curé."

He put forth his hand. "Brother sportsmen," he said. "It *is* a brotherhood, isn't it? You are a Protestant, is it not so?" And his voice sank to a gentle tone.

"Yes, I am what they call a blue Presbyterian."

"I have heard of that," he said. "'A *blue* Presbyterian.'" He repeated it to himself and smiled. Suddenly he straightened and his finger went to his lips.

"Hark!" he whispered. "Hear their wings!"

Instantly the decoys set up a strenuous quacking. Then again all was silent.

"Too high," muttered the curé. "I do not

expect much in before the late afternoon. Do you smoke?"

"Yes, gladly," I replied, "but my cigarettes are done for, I am afraid; they were in the pocket of my hunting coat."

"Don't move," he said, noticing my effort to rise. "I've got cigarettes." And he fumbled in the shadow of the narrow shelf.

I had hardly lighted my own over the candle-flame, which he held for me, when I felt a gentle rocking and heard the shells rattle as they rolled to the end of the shelf, stop, and roll back again.

"Do not be alarmed," he laughed, "it's only the water filling the outer jacket of my *gabion*. We shall be settled and steady in a moment, and afloat for the night."

"The night!" I exclaimed in amazement. "But, my good friend, I have no intention of wearing out my welcome; I had planned to get home for luncheon."

"Impossible!" he replied. "We are now completely surrounded by water. It is always so at high tide at this end of the bay. Come, see for yourself. Besides, you don't know how glad I am that we can have the chance to shoot together. I've been waiting weeks for this wind."

He blew out the candle, and again opened the firing-slit. As far as one could see the distant sea was one vast sweep of roaring water.

"You see," he said, closing the firing-slit and striking a match — "you *must* stay. I have plenty of dry clothes for you in the locker, and we shall not go hungry." He drew out a basket from beneath the cot and took from it a roasted chicken, two litres of red wine, and some bread and cheese, which he laid on the shelf. "A present," he remarked, "from one of my parishioners. You know, I have no *bonne*."

"I have heard so," said I.

He laughed softly. "One hears everything in the village. Ah! But what good children they are! They even forgive my love of shooting!" He crossed his strong arms in the rusty black sleeves of his cassock, and for some moments looked at me seriously. "You think it strange, no doubt, irreverent, for a curé to shoot," he continued. "Forgive me if I have shocked the ideas of your faith."

"Nonsense!" I returned, raising my hand in protest. "You are only human, an honest sportsman. We understand each other perfectly."

"Thank you," he returned, with sincerity. "I was afraid you might not understand — you are the first American I have ever met."

He began taking out an outfit of sailor's clothes from the locker — warm things — which I proceeded to get into with satisfaction. I had just poked my head through the rough jersey and buckled my belt when our decoys again gave warning.

Out went the candle.

"Mallards!" whispered the curé. "Here, take this gun, quick! It is the marquis's favourite," he added in a whisper.

He reached for another breech-loader, motioned me to the chair, let down the three compartments of the firing-slit, and stretched himself out full length on the cot, his keen eyes scanning the bay at a glance.

We were just in time — a dozen mallards were coming straight for our decoys.

Bang! thundered the curé's gun.

Bang! Bang! echoed my own. Then another roar from the curé's left barrel. When the smoke cleared three fat ducks were kicking beyond our deceivers.

"Take him!" he cried, as a straggler — a drake — shot past us. I snapped in a shell and missed, but the curé was surer. Down came the straggler, a dead duck at sixty yards.

"Bravo, Monsieur le Curé!" I cried.

But he only smiled modestly and, extracting the empty shell, blew the lurking smoke free from the barrels. It was noon when we turned to half the chicken and a bottle of *vin ordinaire* with an appetite.

The northeast wind had now shifted to the south; the bay became like glass, and so the afternoon passed until the blood-red sun, like some huge ribbed lantern of the Japanese, slowly sank into the sea. It grew dusk over the desolate marsh. Stray flights of plovers, now that the tide was again on its ebb, began to choose their resting places for the night.

"I'm going out to take a look," said the curé.

Again, like some gopher of the prairie, he rose up out of his burrow.

Presently he returned, the old enthusiastic gleam in his eyes.

"The wind's changing," he announced. "It will be in the north again to-night; we shall have a full moon and better luck, I hope. Do you know," he went on excitedly, "that one night last October I killed forty-two ducks alone in this old *gabion*. *Forty-two!* Twenty mallards and the rest Vignon — and not a shot before one o'clock in the morning. Then they came in, right and left. I believe my faithful decoys will remember that night until their dying day. Ah, it was glorious! Glorious!" His tanned, weather-beaten features wrinkled with delight; he had the skin of a sailor, and I wondered how often the marsh had hid him. "Ah, my friend," he said, with a sigh, as we sat down to the remainder of the chicken and *vin ordinaire* for supper, this time including the cheese, "it is not easy for a curé to shoot. My good children of the village do not mind, but ——" He hesitated, running his long, vibrant fingers through his hair.

"What then? Tell me," I ventured. "It will go no further, I promise you."

"Rome!" he whispered. "I have already received a letter, a gentle warning from the palace; but I have a good friend in Cardinal Z. He understands."

During the whole of that cold moonlight we took turns of two hours each; one sleeping while the other watched in the chair drawn up close to the firing-slit.

What a night!

The marsh seen through the firing-slit, with its overhanging eyebrow of sod, seemed not of this earth. The nine black decoys picketed before us straining at their cords, gossiping. dozing for a moment, preening their wings or rising up for a vigorous stretch, appeared by some curious optical illusion four times their natural size; now they seemed to be black dogs, again a group of sombre, misshapen gnomes.

While I watched, the curé slept soundly, his body shrouded in the blankets like some carved Gothic saint of old. The silence was intense — a silence that could be heard — broken only

by the brisk ticking of the curé's watch on the
narrow shelf. Occasionally a water-rat would
patter over the sunken roof, become inquisitive,
and peer in at me through the slit within half a
foot of my nose. Once in a while I took down
the fat opera-glass, focussing it upon the dim
shapes that resembled ducks, but that proved
to be bits of floating seaweed or a scurrying
shadow as a cloud swept under the moon — all
illusions, until my second watch, when, with a
rush, seven mallards tumbled among our decoys.
Instantly the curé awakened, sprang from his
cot, and with sharp work we killed four.

"Stay where you are," he said as he laid his
gun back in its rack. "I'll get into my hip-
boots and get them before the water-rats steal
what we've earned. They are skilled enough
to get a decoy now and then. The marsh is
alive with them at night."

Morning paled. The village lay half hidden
behind the rifts of mist. Then dawn and the
rising sun, the water like molten gold, the black
decoys churning at their pickets sending up
swirls of turquoise in the gold.

Suddenly the cracked bell rang out from the distant village. At that moment two long V-shaped strings of mallards came winging toward us from the north. I saw the curé glance at them. Then he held out his hand to me.

"You take them — I cannot," he said hurriedly. "I haven't a moment to lose — it is the bell for mass. Here's the key. Lock up when you leave."

"Dine with me to-night," I insisted, one eye still on the incoming ducks. "You have no *bonne*."

His hand was on the *gabion* door. "And if the northeast wind holds," he called back, "shall we shoot again to-night?"

"Yes, to-night!" I insisted.

"Then I'll come to dinner." And the door closed with a click.

Through the firing-slit I could see him leaping across the marsh toward the gray church with the cracked bell, and as he disappeared by the short cut I pulled the trigger of both barrels — and missed.

An hour later Suzette greeted me with eyes full of tears and anxiety.

"Ah! Mother of Pity! Monsieur is safe!" she cried. "Where has monsieur been, *mon Dieu!*"

"To mass, my child," I said gravely, filling her plump arms with the ducks. "Monsieur le Curé is coming to dinner!"

CHAPTER THREE

THE EXQUISITE MADAME DE BRÉVILLE

POOR Tanrade! Just as I felt the future was all *couleur de rose* with him it has changed to gloom unutterable.

Ah, les femmes! I should never dare fall in love with a woman as exquisite as Alice de Bréville. She is too beautiful, too seductive, with her olive skin, her frank smile, and her adorable head poised upon a body much too well made. She is too tender, too complex, too intelligent. She has a way of mischievously caressing you with her eyes one moment and giving an old comrade like myself a platonic little pat on the back the next, which is exasperating. As a friend I adore her, but to fall in love with her! *Ah, non, merci!* I have had a checkered childhood and my full share of suffering; I wish some peace in my old age. At sixteen one goes to the war of love blindly, but at forty it is different. Our chagrins then plunge us into a state of dignified desolation.

Poor Tanrade! I learned of the catastrophe the other night when he solemnly entered my abandoned house by the marsh and sank his big frame in the armchair before my fire. He was no longer the genial bohemian of a Tanrade I had known. He was silent and haggard. He had not slept much for a week; neither had he worked at the score of his new opera or hunted, but he had smoked incessantly, furiously — a dangerous remedy with which to mend a broken heart.

My poor old friend! I was so certain of his happiness that night after dinner here in the House Abandoned, when he and Alice had lost themselves in the moonlight. Was it the moonlight? Or the kiss she gave him as they stood looking out over the lichen-stained wall of the courtyard to the fairy marsh beyond, still and sublime — wedded to the open sea at high tide — like a mirror of polished silver, its surface ruffled now and then by the splash of some incoming duck. He had poured out his heart to her then, and again over their liqueur and cigarettes at that fatal dinner of two at the château.

All this he confessed to me as he sat staring into the cheery blaze on my hearth. Under my friendly but somewhat judicial cross-examination that ensued, it was evident that not a word had escaped Alice's lips that any one but that big optimistic child of a Tanrade could have construed as her promise to be his wife. He confided her words to me reluctantly, now that he realized how little she had meant.

"Come," said I, in an effort to cheer him, "have courage! A woman's heart that is won easily is not worth fighting for. You shall see, old fellow — things will be better."

But he only shook his head, shrugged his great shoulders, and puffed doggedly at his pipe in silence. My tall clock in the corner ticked the louder, its brass pendulum glinting as it swung to and fro in the light of the slumbering fire. I threw on a fresh log, kicked it into a blaze, and poured out for him a stiff glass of applejack. I had faith in that applejack, for it had been born in the moonlit courtyard years ago. It roused him, for I saw something of his old-time self brighten within him; he even made an attempt at a careless smile — the reminiscent smile of a philosopher this time.

"What if I went to see her?" I remarked pointblank.

"You! *Mon Dieu!*" He half sprang out of the armchair in his intensity. "Are you crazy?"

"Forgive me," I apologized. "I did not mean to hurt you. I only thought — and you are in no condition to reason — that Alice may have changed her mind, may regret having refused you. Women change their minds, you know. She might even confess this to me since there is nothing between us and we are old friends."

"No, no," he protested. "You are not to speak of me to Madame de Bréville — do you understand?" he cried, his voice rising. "You are not to mention my name, promise me that."

This time it was I who shrugged my shoulders in reply. He sat gripping the arms of his chair, again his gaze reverted stolidly to the fire. The clock ticked on past midnight, peacefully aloof as if content to be well out of the controversy.

"A drop more?" I ventured, reaching for the decanter; but he stayed my arm.

"I've been a fool," he said slowly. "*Ah! Mon Dieu! Les femmes! Les femmes! Les femmes!*" he roared. "Very well," he exclaimed hotly, "it is well finished. To-morrow I must go to Paris for the new rehearsals. I have begged off for a week. Duclos is beside himself with anxiety — two telegrams to-day, the last one imperative. The new piece must open at the Folies Parisiennes the eighth."

I saw him out to the gate and there was a brave ring in his "*bonsoir, mon vieux,*" as he swung off in the dusk of the starlit road.

He left the village the next day at noon by the toy train, "the little get off-the-track," as we call it. Perhaps he wished it would and end everything, including the rehearsals.

Bah! To be rehearsing lovelorn shepherds

and shepherdesses in sylvan dells. To call
a halt eighteen times in the middle of the
romantic duet between the unhappy innkeeper's
daughter and the prince. To marry them all
smoothly in B flat in the finale, and keep the
brass down and the strings up in the apotheosis
when the heart of the man behind the baton
has been cured of all love and illusion — for
did he not tell me "It is well finished"? Poor
Tanrade!

Though it is but half a fortnight since he
left, it seems years since he used to come into
my courtyard, for he came and went as freely
at all hours as the salt breeze from the marsh.
Often he would wake me at daybreak, bellowing
up to my window at the top of his barytone
lungs some stirring aria, ending with: "Eh,
mon vieux! Stop playing the prince! Get
up out of that and come out on the marsh.
There are ducks off the point. Where's Suzette?
Where's the coffee? *Sacristi!* What a house.
Half-past four and nobody awake!"

And he would stand there grinning; his big
chest encased in a fisherman's jersey, a dis-

reputable felt hat jammed on his head, and his feet in a pair of sabots that clattered like a farm-horse as he went foraging in the kitchen, up-setting the empty milk-tins and making such a bedlam that my good little maid-of-all-work, Suzette, would hurry in terror into her clothes and out to her beloved kitchen to save the rest from ruin.

Needless to say, nothing ever happened to anything. He could make more noise and do less harm than any one I ever knew. Then he would sing us both into good humour until Suzette's peasant cheeks shone like ripe apples.

"It is not the same without Monsieur Tan-rade," Suzette sighed to-day as she brought my luncheon to my easel in a shady corner of my wild garden — a corner all cool roses and shadow.

"Ah, no!" I confessed as I squeezed out the last of a tube of vermilion on the edge of my palette.

"Ah, no!" she sighed softly, and wiped her eyes briskly with the back of her dimpled red hand. "Ah, no! *Parbleu!*"

And just then the bell over my gate jingled. "Some one rings," whispered Suzette and she ran to open the gate. It was the *valet de chambre* from the château with a note from Alice, which read:

DEAR FRIEND: It is lonely, this big house of mine. Do come and dine with me at eight.
                    Hastily,   A. DE B.

Added to this was the beginning of a postscript crossed out.

Upon a leaf torn from my sketchbook I scribbled the answer:

GOOD DEAR CHARITABLE FRIEND: The House Abandoned is a hollow mockery without Tanrade. I'll come gladly at eight.

And Suzette brought it out to the waiting *valet de chambre* whom she addressed respectfully as "monsieur," half on account of his yellow-striped waistcoat and half because he was a Parisian.

Bravo, Alice! Here then was the opportunity I had been waiting for, and I hugged myself over the fact. It was like the first ray of sunshine breaking through a week of leaden sky. For a long time I paced back and forth among the paths of the snug garden, past the roses and the heliotrope down as far as the flaming geraniums and the hollyhocks and the droning bees, and back again by way of some excellent salads and the bed of artichokes, while I turned over in my mind and rehearsed to myself all I intended to say to her.

Alice lonely! With a château, two automobiles, and all Paris at her pretty feet! Ha! ha! The symptoms were excellent. The patient was doing well. To-night would see her convalescent and happily on the road to recovery. This once happy family of comrades should be no longer under the strain of disunion, we should have another dinner soon and the House Abandoned would ring with cheer as it had never rung before. Japanese lanterns among the fruit-trees of the tangled garden, the courtyard full of villagers, red and

blue fire, skyrockets and congratulations, a Normand dinner and a keg of good sound wine to
wish a long and happy life to both.   There
would be the same Tanrade again and the same
Alice, and they would be married by the curé in
the little gray church with the cracked bell,
with the marquis and the marquise as notables
in the front pew.   In my enthusiasm I saw it all.

The lane back of the House Abandoned
shortens the way to the château by half a kilo-
metre.   It was this lane that I entered at dusk
by crawling under the bars that divided it from
the back pasture full of gnarled apple-trees,
under which half a dozen mild-eyed cows had
settled themselves for the night.   They rose
when they caught sight of me and came toward
me blowing deep moist breaths as a quiet chal-
lenge to the intruder, until halted by the bars
they stood in a curious group watching me until
I disappeared up the lane, a lane screened from
the successive pastures on either side by an
impenetrable hedge and flanked its entire
length by tall trees, their tops meeting overhead

like the Gothic arches of a cathedral aisle.
This roof of green made the lane at this hour
so dark that I had to look sharp to avoid the
muddy places, for the lane ascended like the
bed of a brook until it reached the plateau of
woodlands and green fields above, commanding
a sweeping view of marsh and sea below.

Birds fluttered nervously in the hedges,
frightened at my approaching footsteps. A
hare sniffing in the middle of the path flattened
his long ears and sprang into the thicket ahead.
The nightingales in the forest above began
calling to one another. Two doves went skim-
ming out of the leaves over my head. Even a
peacemaker may be mistaken for an enemy.
And now I had gained the plateau and it grew
lighter — that gentle light with which night
favours the open places.

There are two crossroads at the top of the
lane. The left one leads to the hamlet of Beau-
fort le Petit, a sunken cluster of farms ten good
leagues from Pont du Sable; the right one
swings off into the highroad half a mile beyond,
which in turn is met by the private way of the

château skirting the stone wall surrounding the park, which, as early as 1608, served as the idle stronghold of the Duc de Rambutin. It has seen much since then and has stood its ground bravely under the stress of misfortune. The Prussians hammered off two of its towers, and an artillery fire once mowed down some of its oldest trees and wrecked the frescoed ceiling and walls of the salon, setting fire to the south wing, which was never rebuilt and whose jagged and blackened walls the roses and vines have long since lovingly hidden from view.

Alice bought this once splendid feudal estate literally for a song — the song in the second act of Fremier's comedy, which had a long run at the Variétés three years ago, and in which she earned an enviable success and some beautiful bank-notes. Were the Duc de Rambutin alive I am sure he would have presented it to her — shooting forest, stone wall, and all. They say he had an intolerable temper, but was kind to ladies and lap-dogs.

It was not long before I unlatched a moss-covered gate with one hinge lost in the weeds

— a little woebegone gate for intimate friends, that croaked like a night-bird when it opened, and closed with a whine. Beyond it lay a narrow path through a rose-garden leading to the château. This rose-garden is the only cultivated patch within the confines of the wall, for on either side of it tower great trees, their aged trunks held fast in gnarled thickets of neglected vines. It is only another "house abandoned," this château of Alice's, save that its bygone splendour asserts itself through the scars, and my own by the marsh never knew luxury even in its best days.

"Madame is dressing," announced that most faithful of old servitors, Henri, who before Alice conferred a full-fledged butlership upon him in his old age was since his youth a stage-carpenter at the Théâtre Français.

"Will monsieur have the goodness to wait for madame in the library?" added Henri, as he relieved me of my hat and stick, deposited them noiselessly upon an oak table, and led me to a portière of worn Gobelin which he lifted for me with a bow of the Second Empire.

What a rich old room it is, this silent library of the choleric duke, with its walls panelled in worm-eaten oak reflecting the firelight and its rows of volumes too close to the grave to be handled.   Here and there above the high wainscoting are ancestral portraits, some of them as black as a favourite pipe.   Above the great stone chimney-piece is a full-length figure of the duke in a hunting costume of green velvet. The candelabra that Henri had just lighted on the long centre-table, littered with silver souvenirs and the latest Parisian comedies, now illumined the duke's smile, which he must have held with bad grace during the sittings.   The rest of him was lost in the shadow above the chimney-piece of sculptured cherubs, whose missing noses have been badly restored in cement by the gardener.

I had settled myself in a chintz-covered chair and was idly turning the pages of one of the latest of the Parisian comedies when I heard the swish of a gown and the patter of two small slippered feet hurrying across the hall. I rose to regard my hostess with a feeling of tender curiosity mingled with resentment over her treatment of my old friend, when the portière was lifted and Alice came toward me with both white arms outstretched in welcome. She was so pale in her dinner gown of black tulle that all the blood seemed to have taken refuge in her lips—so pale that the single camellia thrust in her corsage was less waxen in its whiteness than her neck.

I caught her hands and she stood close to me, smiling bravely, the tips of her fingers trembling in my own.

"You are ill!" I exclaimed, now thoroughly alarmed. "You must go straight to bed."

"No, no," she replied, with an effort. "Only tired, very tired."

"You should not have let me come," I protested.

She smiled and smoothed back a wave of her glossy black hair and I saw the old mischievous gleam flash in her dark eyes.

"Come," she whispered, leading me to the door of the dining room. "It is a secret," she confided, with a forced little laugh. "Look!" And she pinched my arm.

I glanced within — the table with its lace and silver under the glow of the red candle-shades was laid for two.

"It was nice of you," I said.

"We shall dine alone, you and I," she murmured. "I am so tired of company."

I was on the point of impulsively mentioning poor Tanrade's absence, but the subtle look in her eyes checked me. During dinner we should have our serious little talk, I said to myself as we returned to the library table.

"It's so amusing, that little comedy of Flandrean's," laughed Alice, picking up the volume I had been scanning. "The second act is a jewel with its delicious situation in which François Villers, the husband, and Thérèse, his wife, divorce in order to carry out between them a secret love-affair — a series of mysterious rendezvous that terminate in an amusing elopement. *Très chic*, Flandrean's comedy. It should have a *succès fou* at the Palais Royal."

"Madame is served," gravely announced Henri.

Not once during dinner was Alice serious.

Over the soup — an excellent bisque of *écrevis-ses* — she bubbled over with the latest Parisian gossip, the new play at the Odéon, the fashion in hats. With the fish she prattled on over the limitations of the new directoire gowns and the scandal involving a certain tenor and a duchess. Tanrade's defence, which I had so carefully thought out and rehearsed in my garden, seemed doomed to remain unheard, for her cleverness in evading the subject, her sudden change to the merriest of moods, and her quick wit left me helpless. Neither did I make any better progress during the pheasant and the salad, and as she sipped but twice the Pommard and scarcely moistened her lips with the champagne my case seemed hopeless. Henri finally left us alone over our coffee and cigarettes. I had become desperate.

"Alice," I said bluntly, "we are old friends. I have some things to say to you of — of the utmost importance. You will listen, my friend, will you not, until I am quite through, for I shall not mention it again?"

She leaned forward with a little start and

gazed at me suddenly with dilated eyes — eyes
that were the next minute lowered in painful
submission, the corners of her mouth contracting
nervously.

"*Mon Dieu!*" she murmured, looking up.
"*Mon Dieu!* But you are cruel!"

"No," I replied calmly. "It is you who are
cruel."

"No, no, you shall not!" she exclaimed,
raising both ringless hands in protest, her breath
coming quick. "I — I know what you are
going to say. No, my dear friend — I beg of
you — we are good comrades. Is it not so?
Let us remain so."

"Listen," I implored.

"Ah, you men with your idea of marriage!"
she continued. "The wedding, the aunts, the
cousins, who come staring at you for a day and
giving you advice for years. A solemn apartment near the Etoile — madame with her
afternoons — monsieur with his club, his maît-
resse, his gambling and his debts — the children
with their English governess. A villa by the
sea, tennis, infants and sand-forts. The annual

stupid *voyage en Suisse*.   The inane slavery of
it all.   *You* who are a bohemian, you who *live*
— with all your freedom — all my freedom!
Non, merci!   I have seen all that!   Bah!   You
are as crazy as Tanrade."

"Alice," I cried, "you think ——"

"Precisely, my friend."

She rose swiftly, crossed the room, and before
I knew it slipped back of my chair, put both
arms about my neck, kissed me, and burst
into tears.

"There, there, *mon pauvre petit*," she whispered.   "Forgive me — I was angry — we are
not so stupid as all that — eh?   We are not
like the stupid *bourgeoisie*."

"But it is not I ——"   I stammered.

She caught her breath in surprise, straightened, and slowly retraced her steps to her vacant
chair.

"Ah!   So it is that?" she said slowly, drawing her chair close to my own.   Then she seated
herself, rested her chin in her hands, and
regarded me for some moments intently.

"So you have come for — for him?" she

resumed, her breast heaving. "I am right, am I not?"

"He loves you," I declared. "Do you think I am blind as to your love for him? You who came to greet me to-night out of your suffering?"

For some moments she was silent, her fingers pressed over her eyes.

"Do you love him?" I insisted.

"No, no," she moaned. "It is impossible."

"Do you know," I continued, "that he has not slept or hunted or smoked for a week before he was forced to go to Paris? Can you realize what he suffers now during days of exhausting rehearsals? He came to me a wreck," I said. "You have been cruel and you have ——"

Again she had become deathly pale. Then at length she rose slowly, lifted her head proudly, and led the way back to the library fire.

"You must go," she said. "It is late."

When the little boy of the fisherman, Jean Tranchard, was not to be found playing with the other barelegged tots in the mud of the village alleys, or wandering alone on the marsh, often dangerously near the sweep of the incoming tide, one could be quite sure he was safe with Tanrade. Frequently, too, when the maker of ballets was locked in his domain and his servant had strict orders to admit no one — neither Monsieur le Curé nor the mayor, nor so intimate a comrade as myself — during such hours as these the little boy was generally beside the composer, his chubby toes scarcely reaching to the rungs of the chair beside Tanrade's working desk.

Though the little boy was barely seven he was a sturdy little chap with fair curly hair, blue eyes, and the quick gestures of his father. He had a way of throwing out his chest when he was pleased, and gesticulating with open arms and closed fists when excited, which is peculiar to the race of fishermen. The only time when he was perfectly still was when Tanrade worked in silence. He would then often sit beside him for hours waiting until the composer dropped his pen, swung round in his chair to the keyboard at his elbow, and while the piano rang with melody the little boy's eyes danced. He forgot during such moments of ecstasy that his father was either out at sea with his nets or back in the village good-naturedly drunk, or that his mother, whom he vaguely remembered, was dead.

Tanrade was a so much better father to him than his own that the rest of his wretched little existence did not count. When the father was fishing, the little boy cared for himself. He knew how to heat the pot and make the soup when there was any to make. He knew where to dig for clams and sputtering crabs. It was the bread that bothered him most — it cost two sous. It was Tanrade who discovered and softened these hard details.

The house in which the fisherman and the little boy live is tucked away in an angle of the walled lane leading out to the marsh. This stone house of Tranchard's takes up as little room as possible, since its front dare not encroach upon the lane and its back is hunched up apologetically against the angle of the wall. The house has but two compartments — the loft above stored with old nets and broken oars, and the living room beneath, whose dirt floor dampens the feet of an oak cupboard, a greasy table, a chair with a broken leg, and a mahogany bed. Over the soot-blackened chimney-piece is a painted figure of the Virgin, and a frigate in a bottle.

Monsieur le Curé had been watching all night beside the mahogany bed. Now and then he slipped his hand in the breast of his soutane of rusty black, drew out a steel watch, felt under a patchwork-quilt for a small feverish wrist, counted its feeble pulse, and filling a pewter spoon with a mixture of aconite, awakened the little boy who gazed at him with hollow eyes sunken above cheeks of dull crimson.

In the corner, his back propped against the cupboard, his bare feet tucked under him, dozed Tranchard. There was not much else he could do, for he was soaked to the skin and half drunk. Occasionally he shifted his feet, awakened, and dimly remembered the little boy was worse; that this news had been hailed to him by the skipper of the mackerel smack, *La Belle Élise*, and that he had hauled in his empty nets and come home.

As the gray light of dawn crept into the room, the little boy again grew restless. He opened the hollow eyes and saw dimly the black figure of the curé.

"Tanné," he whimpered. "Where is he, Tanné?"

"Monsieur Tanrade will come," returned the curé, "if you go to sleep like a brave little man."

"Tanné," repeated the child and closed his eyes obediently.

A cock crowed in a distant yard, awakening a sleek cat who emerged from beneath the bed, yawned, stretched her claws, and walked out of the narrow doorway into the misty lane.

The curé rose stiffly, went over to the figure in the corner and shook it. Tranchard started up out of a sound sleep.

"Tell madame when she arrives that I have gone for Doctor Thévenet. I shall return before night."

"I won't forget," grumbled Tranchard.

"I have left instructions for madame beside the candle. See that you keep the kettle boiling for the poultices."

The fisherman nodded. "*Eh ben!* How is it with the kid?" he inquired. "He does not take after his mother. *Parbleu!* She was as strong as a horse, my woman."

Monsieur le Curé did not reply. He had taken down his flat black hat from a peg and was carefully adjusting his square black cravat edged with white beneath his chin, when Alice de Bréville entered the doorway.

"How is his temperature?" she asked eagerly, unpinning a filmy green veil and throwing aside a gray automobile coat.

Monsieur le Curé graciously uncovered his head. "There has been no change since you left at midnight," he said gravely. "The fever is still high, the pulse weaker. I am going for Doctor Thévenet after mass. There is a train at eight."

Tranchard was now on his knees fanning a pile of fagots into a blaze, the acrid smoke drifting back into the low-ceiled room.

"I will attend to it," said Alice, turning to the fisherman. "Tell my chauffeur to wait at the church for Monsieur le Curé. The auto is at the end of the lane."

For some minutes after the clatter of Tranchard's sabots had died away in the lane, Alice de Bréville and Monsieur le Curé stood in earnest conversation beside the table.

"It may save the child's life," pleaded the priest. There was a ring of insistence in his voice, a gleam in his eyes that made the woman beside him tremble.

"You do not understand," she exclaimed, her breast heaving. "You do not realize what you ask of me. I cannot."

"You must," he insisted. "He might not understand it coming from me. You and he are old friends. You *must*, I tell you. Were he only here the child would be happy, the fever would be broken. It must be broken and quickly. Thévenet will tell you that when he comes."

Alice raised her hands to her temples.

"Will you?" he pleaded.

"Yes," she replied half audibly.

Monsieur le Curé gave a sigh of relief.

"God be with you!" said he.

He watched her as she wrote in haste the

following telegram in pencil upon the back of
a crumpled envelope:

MONSIEUR TANRADE, Théâtre des Folies Parisi-
    ennes, Paris.
Tranchard's child very ill.   Come at once.
                              A. DE BRÉVILLE.

This she handed to the priest in silence.
Monsieur le Curé tucked it safely in the
breast of his cassock. "God be with you!" he
repeated and turned out into the lane. He
ran, for the cracked bell for mass had ceased
ringing.

The woman stood still by the table as if in a
dream, then she staggered to the door, closed it,
and throwing herself on her knees by the bed-
side of the sleeping boy, buried her face in her
hands.

The child stirred, awakened by her sobbing.

"Tanné," he cried feebly.

"He will come," she said.

Outside in the mist-soaked lane three tooth-
less fisherwomen gossiped in whispers.

Almost any day that you pass through the village you will see a chubby little rascal who greets you with a cheery *"Bonjour"* and runs away, dragging a tin horse with a broken tail. Should you chance to glance over my wall you will discover the tattered remnants of two Japanese lanterns hanging among the fruit-trees. They are all that remain of a fête save the memory of two friends to whom the whole world now seems *couleur de rose*.

"Hi, there! wake up! Where's Suzette? Where's the coffee! Daylight and not a soul up! *Mon Dieu*, what a house! Hurry up, *Mon vieux!* Alice is waiting!"

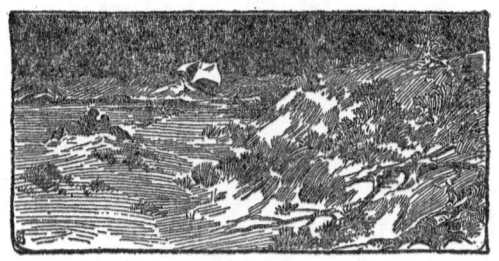

CHAPTER FOUR

SOME centuries ago the windows of my house abandoned on the marsh looked out upon a bay gay with the ships of Spanish pirates, for in those days Pont du Sable served them as a secret refuge for repairs. Hauled up to the tawny marsh were strange craft with sails of apple-green, rose, vermilion and sinister black; there were high sterns pierced by carved cabin-windows — some of them iron-barred, to imprison ladies of high or low degree and unfortunate gentlemen who fought bravely to defend them. From oaken gunwales glistened slim cannon, their throats swabbed clean after some wholesale murder on the open seas. Yes, it must have been a lively enough bay some centuries ago!

To-day Pont du Sable goes to bed without even turning the key in the lock.   This is because of a vast army of simple men whose word, in France, is law.

To begin with, there are the President of the République and the Ministers of War and Agriculture, and Monsieur the Chief of Police — a kind little man in Paris whom it is better to agree with — and the préfet and the sous-préfet — all the way down the line of authority to the red-faced, blustering *chef de gare* at Pont du Sable — and Pierre.

On off-duty days Pierre is my gardener at eleven sous an hour.   On these occasions he wears voluminous working trousers of faded green corduroy gathered at the ankles; a gray flannel shirt and a scarlet cravat.   On other days his short, wiry body is encased in a carefully brushed uniform of dark blue with a double row of gold buttons gleaming down his solid chest.   When on active duty in the Customs Coast Patrol of the République Française at Pont du Sable, he carries a neatly folded cape with a hood, a bayonet, a heavy calibred six-shooter and a trusty field-glass, useful in locating suspicious-looking objects on marsh or sea.

On this particular morning Pierre was late! I had been leaning over the lichen-stained wall of my wild garden waiting to catch sight of him as he left the ragged end of the straggling village. Had I mistaken the day? Impossible! It was Thursday and I knew he was free. Finally I caught sight of him hurrying toward me down the road — not in his working clothes of faded green corduroy, but in the full majesty of his law-enforcing uniform. What had happened? I wondered. Had his stern brigadier refused to give him leave?

"*Bonjour*, Pierre!" I called to him as he came within hailing distance.

He touched the vizor of his cap in military salute, and a moment later entered my garden.

"A thousand pardons, monsieur," he apologized excitedly, labouring to catch his breath.

"My artichokes have been waiting for you," I laughed; "they are nearly strangled with weeds. I expected you yesterday." He followed me

through a lane of yellow roses leading to the arti-
choke bed. "What has kept you, Pierre?"

He stopped, looked me squarely in the eyes,
placed his finger in the middle of his spiked
moustache, and raised his eyebrows mysteriously.

"Monsieur must not ask me," he replied. "I
have been on duty for forty-eight hours; there
was not even time to change my uniform."

"A little matter for headquarters?" I ventured
indiscreetly, with a nod in the direction of Paris.

Pierre shrugged his shoulders and smiled.
"Monsieur must ask the semaphore; my lips
are sealed."

Had he been the chief of the Secret Service
just in possession of the whereabouts of an inter-
national criminal, he could not have been more
uncommunicative.

"And monsieur's artichokes?" he asked,
abruptly changing the subject.

Further inquiry I knew was useless — even
dangerous. Indeed I swallowed my curiosity
whole, for I was aware that this simple gardener
of mine, in his official capacity, could put me in
irons, drag me before my friend the ruddy little

mayor, and cast me in jail at Bar la Rose, had
I given him cause. Then indeed, as Pom-
panet said, I would be "A *sacré* vagabond from
Pont du Sable."

Was it not only the other day a well-dressed
stranger hanging about my lost village had been
called for by two gendarmes, owing to Pierre's
watchful eye? And did not the farmer Milon
pay dearly enough for the applejack he distilled
one dark night? I recalled, too, a certain morning when, a stranger on the marsh, I had lighted
Pierre's cigarette with an honest wax-match
from England. He recognized the brand instantly.

"They are the best in the world," I had
remarked bravely.

"Yes," he had replied, "but dear, monsieur.
The fine is a franc apiece in France."

We had reached the artichokes.

"*Mon Dieu!*" exclaimed Pierre, glancing at
the riot of weeds as he stripped off his coat and,
unbuckling his belt with the bayonet, the six-
shooter and the field-glass, hung them in the
shade upon a convenient limb of a pear tree. He

measured the area of the unruly patch with a military stride, stood thinking for a moment, and then, as if a happy thought had struck him, returned to me with a gesture of enthusiasm.

"If monsieur will permit me to offer a suggestion — that is, if monsieur approves — I should like to make a fresh planting. Ah! I will explain what I mean to monsieur, so monsieur may see clearly my ideas. *Voilà!*" he exclaimed. "It is to have the new artichokes planted in three circles — in three circles, monsieur," he went on excitedly, "crossed with the star of the compass," he continued, as the idea rapidly developed in his peasant brain. "Then in the centre of the star to plant monsieur's initials in blue and red flowers. *Voilà!* It will be something for monsieur's friends to admire, eh?"

He stood waiting tensely for my reply, for I shivered inwardly at the thought of the prospective chromo.

"Excellent, my good Pierre," I returned, not wishing to hurt his feelings. "Excellent for the gardens of the Tuileries, but my garden is such a simple one."

"Pardon, monsieur," he said, with a touch of mingled disappointment and embarrassment, "they shall be replanted, of course, just as monsieur wishes." And Pierre went to digging weeds with a will while I went back to my own work.

At noon Pierre knocked gently at my study door.

"I must breakfast, monsieur," he apologized, "and get a little sleep. I have promised my brigadier to get back at three."

"And to-morrow?" I asked.

Again the shoulders shrugged under the uniform.

"Ah, monsieur!" he exclaimed helplessly. "*Malheureusement,* to-morrow I am not free; nor the day after. *Parbleu!* I cannot tell monsieur *when* I shall be free."

"I understand, Pierre," said I.

Before sundown the next afternoon I was after a hare through a maze of thicket running back of the dunes fronting the open sea. I kept on through a labyrinth of narrow trails — cross-

ing and recrossing each other — the private
by-ways of sleek old hares in time of trouble, for
the dunes were honeycombed with their bur-
rows. Now and then I came across a tent-
shaped thatched hut lined with a bed of straw,
serving as snug shelters for the coast patrol in
tough weather.

I had just turned into a tangle of scrub-brush,
and could hear the breakers pound and hiss as
they swept up upon the hard smooth beach
beyond the dunes, when a low whistle brought
me to a leisurely halt, and I saw Pierre spring
up from a thicket a rod ahead of me — a Government carbine nestled in the hollow of his arm.

I could scarcely believe it was the genial and
ever-willing Pierre of my garden. He was the
hard-disciplined soldier now, under orders. I
was thankful he had not sent a bullet through
me for not halting more promptly than I did.

"What are you doing here?" he demanded,
coming briskly toward me along a trail no wider
than his feet.

Instantly my free hand went to my hunting-
cap in salute.

"After — a— hare!" I stammered innocently.

"Not so loud," he whispered. "*Mon Dieu!* If the brigadier should hear you! Come with me," he commanded, laying his hand firmly upon my arm. "There are six of us hidden between here and the fortress. It is well that you stumbled upon me first. They must know who you are. It is not safe for you to be hunting to-day."

I had not followed him more than a dozen rods before one of his companions was at my side. "The American," said Pierre in explanation, and we passed on down through a riot of stunted growth that choked the sides of a hollow.

Beyond this rose the top of a low circular fort overgrown with wire-grass — the riot of tangle ceasing as we reached the bottom of the hollow and stood in an open patch before an ancient iron gate piercing the rear of the fort.

Pierre lifted the latch and we passed through a wall some sixteen feet thick and into a stone-paved courtyard with a broad flight of steps at its farther end sweeping to the top of the circular defence. Flanking the sunken courtyard itself were a dozen low vaultlike compartments, some

of them sealed by heavy doors.   At one of these,
containing a narrow window, Pierre knocked.
The door opened and I stood in the presence of
the Brigadier Bompard.

"The   American   gentleman," announced
Pierre, relieving me of my gun.

The brigadier bowed, looked me over sharply,
and bade me enter.

"At your service, monsieur," he said coldly,
waving his big freckled hand toward a chair
drawn up to a fat little stove blushing under a
forced draft.

"At yours, monsieur," I returned, bowed, and
took my seat.

Then there ensued a dead silence, Pierre standing rigid behind my chair, the brigadier reseated
back of a desk littered with official papers.

For some moments he sat writing, his savage
gray eyes scanning the page, the ends of his
ferocious moustache twitching nervously as his
pen scratched on.   Back of his heavy shoulders
ran a shelf supporting a row of musty ledgers,
and above a stout chest in one corner was a rack
of gleaming carbines.

The silence became embarrassing. Still the pen scratched on. Was he writing my death-warrant, I wondered nervously, or only a milder order for my arrest? It was a relief when he finally sifted a spoonful of fine blue sand over the document, poured the remaining grains back into their receptacle, puffed out his coarse red jowls, emitted a grunt of approval, and raised his keen eyes to mine.

"A thousand pardons, monsieur," I began, "for being where I assure you I would not have been had I known exactly where I was."

"So monsieur is fond of the chase of the hare?" he asked, with a grim smile.

"So fond, Monsieur le Brigadier," I replied, "that my enthusiasm has, as you see, led me thoughtlessly into your private territory. I beg of you to accept my sincere apologies."

He reached back of him, took down one of the musty ledgers, and began to turn the leaves methodically. From where I sat I saw his coarse forefinger stop under a head-line.

"Smeeth, Berkelek," he muttered, and read

on down the page. "Citizen of *Amérique du Nord*.

"Height — medium.

"Age — forty-one.

"Hair — auburn.

"Eyes — brown.

"Chin and frontal — square.

"No scars."

"Would your excellency like to see my hunting permit and description?" I ventured.

"Unnecessary — it is in duplicate here," he returned curtly, and his eyes again reverted to the ledger. Then he closed the book, rose, and drawing his chair to the stove planted his big fists on his knees.

I began to breathe normally.

"So you are a painter?" said he.

"Yes," I confessed, "but I do not make a specialty of fortresses, your excellency, even in the most distant landscapes."

I was grateful he understood, for I saw a gleam of merriment flash in his eyes.

"*Bon!*" he exclaimed briskly — evidently the title of "excellency" helped. "It is not the best day, however, for you to be hunting hares. Are you a good shot, monsieur?"

"That is an embarrassing question," I returned. "If I do not miss I generally kill."

Pierre, who, during the interview, had been standing mute in attention, now stepped up to him and bending with a hurried "Pardon," whispered something in his coarse red ear.

The brigadier raised his shaggy eyebrows and nodded in assent.

"Ah! So you are a friend of Monsieur le Curé!" he exclaimed. "You would not be Monsieur le Curé's friend if you were not a good shot. *Sapristi!*" He paused, ran his hand over his rough jowls, and resumed bluntly: "It is something to kill the wild duck; another to kill a man."

"Has war been suddenly declared?" I asked in astonishment.

A gutteral laugh escaped his throat, he shook his grizzled head in the negative.

"A little war of my own," said he, "a serious business, *parbleu!*"

"Contraband?" I ventured.

The coarse mouth under the bristling moustache, four times the size of Pierre's, closed with a snap, then opened with a growl.

"*Sacré mille tonnerres!*" he thundered, slamming his fist down on the desk within reach of him. "They are the devil, those Belgians! It is for them my good fellows lose their sleep." Then he stopped, and eyeing me shrewdly added: "Monsieur, you are an outsider and a gentleman. I can trust you. Three nights ago a strange sloop, evidently Belgian, from the cut of her, tried to sneak in here, but our semaphore on the point held her up and she had to run back to the open sea. Bah! Those *sacré* Belgians have the patience of a fox!"

"She was painted like one of our fishing-smacks," interposed Pierre, now too excited to hold his tongue, "but she did not know the channel."

"Aye, and she'll try it again," growled the brigadier, "if the night be dark. She'll find it clear sailing in, but a hot road out."

"Tobacco?" I asked, now fully alive to the situation.

The brigadier spat.

"Of course, as full as she'll float," he answered. He leaned forward and touched me good-humouredly on the shoulder. "I'm short of men," he said hurriedly.

"Command me," I replied. "I'll do my best. I shall return to-night." And I rose to take my leave, but he instantly raised his hand in protest. "You are under arrest, monsieur," he declared quietly, with a shrug of his shoulders.

I looked at him wide-eyed in astonishment. "Arrest!" I gasped.

"Do not be alarmed," he replied. "It will only be temporary, I assure you, but since you have so awkwardly stumbled among us there is no alternative but for me to detain you until this *sacré* affair is well over. I cannot, at all events, let you return to the village to-night."

"But I give you my word of honour, monsieur," I declared, "I shall not open my lips to a soul. Besides, I must dine at eight to-night with Madame de Bréville. Your excellency can well understand."

"I know you have friends, monsieur; they

might be inquisitive; and those friends have servants, and those servants have friends," was his reply. "No, it is better that you stay. Pierre, give monsieur a carbine and a place ten metres from your own at sundown; then report to me he is there. Now you may go, monsieur."

Pierre touched me on the shoulder; then suddenly realizing I was under orders and a prisoner, I straightened, saluted the brigadier, and followed Pierre out of the fort with the best grace I could muster.

"Pierre!" I exclaimed hotly, as we stood again in the thicket. "How long since you've held up anything here — contraband, I mean?"

For a moment he hesitated, then his voice sank to a whisper.

"They say it is all of twenty years, perhaps longer," he confessed. "But to-night monsieur shall see. Monsieur is, of course, not exactly a prisoner or he would now be in the third vault from the right."

"A prisoner! The devil I'm not? Didn't he tell me I was?" I exclaimed.

"*Mon Dieu!* What will you have, monsieur ?"
returned Pierre excitedly, under his breath.
"It is the brigadier's orders. I was afraid
monsieur might reply to him in anger. Ah, *par
exemple!* Then monsieur would have seen a
wild bull. Oh, la! la! When the brigadier is
furious —— Ah, *ça!*" And he led the way
to my appointed ambush without another word.

Despite my indignation at being thus forced
into the service and made a prisoner to boot —
however temporary it might be — I gradually
began to see the humour of the situation. It was
very like a comic opera, I thought, as I lay flat
on the edge of the thicket and pried away a small
opening in the tangle through which I could
look down upon the sweep of beach below me
and far out to sea. Thus I lay in wait for the
smuggling crew to arrive — to be blazed at and
perhaps captured.

What if they outnumber us? We might all
perish then, with no hope of quarter from these
men whom we were lying in wait for like snakes
in the grass. One thing, however, I was firmly
resolved upon, and that was to shoot safely over

anything that lay in range except in case of self-defence. I was never of a murderous disposition, and the thought of another's blood on my hands sent a fresh shiver along my prostrate spine. Then again the comic-opera side of it struck me. I began to feel more like an extra super in a one-night stand than a real soldier. What, after all, if the smugglers failed us?

I was pondering upon the dangerous effect upon the brigadier of so serious a stage wait, when Pierre crawled over to me from his ambush ten metres from my own, to leave me my ration of bread and wine. He was so excited by this time that his voice trembled in my ear.

"Gaston, my comrade, the fifth down the line," he whispered, "has just seen two men prowling on the marsh; they are, without doubt, accomplices. Gaston has gone to tell the brigadier." He ran his hand carefully along the barrel of my carbine. "Monsieur must hold high," he explained in another whisper, "since monsieur is unaccustomed to the gun of war. It is this little machine here that does the trick." He bent his eyes close to the hind sight and screwed it up to its notch at one hundred and fifty metres.

I nodded my thanks, and he left me to my bread and wine and crept cautiously back to his ambush.

A black night was rapidly settling. Above me in the great unfathomable vault of sky not a star glimmered. Under the gloom of the approaching darkness the vast expanse of marsh to my left lay silent, desolate, and indistinct, save for its low edge of undulating sand dunes. Only the beach directly before me showed plainly, seemingly illumined by the breakers, that gleamed white like the bared teeth of a fighting line of wolves.

It was a sullen, cheerless sea, from which the air blew over me damp and raw; the only light visible being the intermittent flash from the distant lighthouse on Les Trois Loups, beyond the marsh.

One hour passed — two hours — during which I saw nothing alive and moving save a hare foraging timidly on the beach for his own rations.

After a while he hopped back to his burrow in the thicket, a thicket of silence from which I knew at any moment might break forth a murderous fire. It grew colder and colder, I had to breathe lustily into the collar of my jersey to keep out the chill. I began to envy the hare snug in his burrow. Thus I held my vigil, and the night wore on.

Ah! my friend the curé! I mused. Was there ever such an indefatigable sportsman? Lucky curé! He was not a prisoner, neither had he been pressed into the customs patrol like a hired assassin. At that moment I knew Monsieur le Curé was snug in his duck-blind for the night, a long two miles from where I lay; warm, and comfortable, with every chance on such a night to kill a dozen fat mallards before his daylight mass.   What would my friend Madame Alice de Bréville, and that whole-souled fellow Tanrade, think when I did not appear as I had promised, at madame's château, to dine at eight? Cold as I was, I could not help chuckling over the fact that it was no fault of mine.

I was a prisoner.   Alice and Tanrade would

dine together. It would be then a dinner for
two. I have never known a woman as discreet as Alice. She had insisted that I dine
with them. In Paris Alice might not have
insisted, but in the lost village, with so many
old women with nothing to talk about save other
peoples' affairs! Lucky Tanrade!

I could see from where I lay the distant mass
of trees screening her château, and picture to
myself my two dear friends *alone*. Their chairs
— now that my vacant one was the only witness
— drawn close together; he holding her soft,
responsive little hand between the soup and the
fish, between the duck and the salad; then con-
tinuously over their dessert and Burgundy —
she whom he had held close to his big heart that
night after dinner in that once abandoned house
of mine, when they had gone out together into
my courtyard and disappeared in the shadows
of the moonlight.

Dining alone! The very thing I had tried to
bring about. But for the stern brigadier we
should have been that wretched number —
three — to-night at the château. Ah, you dear

human children, are you conscious and grateful
that I am lying out like a vagabond, a prisoner,
that you may be alone?

I began to wonder, too, what the Essence of
Selfishness, that spoiled and adorable cat of mine,
would think when it came her bedtime hour.
Would Suzette, in her anxiety over my absence,
remember to give her the saucer of warm milk?
Yet I knew the Essence of Selfishness would take
care of herself; she would sleep with Suzette.
Catch her lying out on the bare ground like her
master when she could curl herself up at the foot
of two fuzzy blankets in a tiny room next to the
warm kitchen.

It was after midnight when Pierre crawled
over to me again, and pointed to a black patch
of mussel rocks below.

"There are the two men Gaston saw," he
whispered. "They are waiting to signal the
channel to their comrades."

I strained my eyes in the direction he indicated.

"I cannot see," I confessed.

"Here, take the glass," said he. "Those two humps behind the big one are the backs of men. They have a lantern well hidden — you can see its glow when the glass is steady."

I could see it all quite clearly now, and occasionally one of the humps lift a head cautiously above the rock.

"She must be lying off close by," muttered Pierre, hoarse with excitement. Again he hurriedly ran his hand over the breech of my carbine. "The trigger pulls light," he breathed. "Courage, monsieur! We have not long to wait now." And again he was gone.

I felt like a hired assassin weakening on the verge of a crime. The next instant I saw the lantern hidden on the mussel rocks raised and lowered thrice.

It was the signal!

Again all was darkness save the gleaming line of surf. My heart thumped in my ears. Ten minutes passed; then again the lantern was raised, the figures of the two men standing in silhouette against its steady rays.

I saw now a small sloop rear itself from the

breakers, a short, squat little craft with a ghostly sail and a flapping jib. On she came, leaping and dropping broadside among the combers. The lantern now shone as clearly as a beacon. A sea broke over the sloop, but she staggered up bravely, and with a plunge was swept nearer and nearer the jagged point of rocks awash with spume. Braced against the tiller was a man in drenched tarpaulins; two other men were holding on to the shrouds like grim death. On the narrow deck between them I made out a bale-like bundle wrapped in tarpaulin and heavily roped, ready to be cast ashore.

A moment more, and the sloop would be on the rocks; yet not a sound came from the thicket. The suspense was sickening. I had once experienced buck-fever, but it was nothing compared to this. The short carbine began to jump viciously under my grip.

The sloop was nearly on the rocks! At that critical moment overboard went the bundle, the two men with the lantern rushing out and dragging it clear of the swash.

Simultaneously, with a crackling roar, six

tongues of flame spat from the thicket and we charged out of our ambush and over the crest of the dunes toward the smugglers' craft and its crew, firing as we ran. The fellow next to me stumbled and fell sprawling in the sand.

In the panic that ensued I saw the sloop making a desperate effort to put to sea. Meanwhile the two accomplices were running like rabbits for the marsh. Close to the mysterious bundle their lantern lay smashed and burning luridly in its oil. The brigadier sprang past me swearing like a pirate, while his now thoroughly demoralized henchmen and myself stumbled on, firing at random with still a good hundred yards between us and the abandoned contraband.

At that instant I saw the sloop's sail fill and then, as if by a miracle, she slowly turned back to the open sea. Above the general din the brigadier's voice rang out, bellowing his orders. By the time the sloop had cleared the breakers his language had become unprintable. He had reached the mussel rocks and stood shaking his clenched fists at the departing craft, while the rest of us crowded about the bundle and the blazing lantern.   Every one was talking and gesticulating at once as they watched the sloop plunge away in the darkness.

"*Sacré mille tonnerres!*" roared the brigadier, sinking down on the bundle.   Then he turned and glared at me savagely.   "Idiot!" he cried, labouring for his breath.   "*Espèce d'imbécile. Ah! Nom d'un petit bonhomme.* You were on the end.   Why did you not head off those devils with the lantern?"

I shrugged my shoulders helplessly in reply. He was in no condition to argue with.

"And the rest of you ——"   He choked in his rage, unable to frame his words.   They stood helplessly about, gesticulating their apologies.

He sprang to his feet, gave the bundle a sound kick, and snarled out an order.   Pierre and another jumped forward, and together they shouldered it between them.   Then the remainder of the valiant guard fell into single file and started back to the fort, the brigadier and myself bringing up the rear.   As we trudged on through the sand together he kept muttering to himself. It only occurred to me then that nobody had been hit. By this time even the accomplices were safe.

"Monsieur," I ventured, as we regained the trail leading to the fort, "it is with the sincerest regret of my heart that I offer you my apologies. True, I might have done better, but I did my best in my inexperience. We have the contraband — at least that is something, eh?"

He grew calmer as the thought struck him.

"Yes," he grumbled, "there are in that bundle at least ten thousand cigars. It is, after all, not so bad."

"Might I ask," I returned, "when your excellency intends to honour me with my liberty?"

He stopped, and to my delight held out his hand to me.

"You are free, monsieur," he said roughly with a touch of his good nature. "The affair is over — but not a word of the manœuvre you have witnessed in the village. Our work here is for the ears of the Government alone."

As we reached the gate of the fort I saluted him, handed my carbine to Pierre in exchange for my shotgun, and struck home in the mist of early dawn.

The morning after, I was leaning over the lichen-stained wall of my garden caressing the white throat of the Essence of Selfishness, the events of my night of service still in my mind, when I saw the coast patrol coming across the marsh in double file. As they drew nearer I recognized Pierre and his companion, who had shouldered the contraband. The roped bundle was swung on a stout pole between them.

Presently they left the marsh and gained the road. As the double file of uniformed men came past my wall they returned my salute. Pierre shifted his end of the pole to the man behind him and stood at attention until the rest had passed. Then the procession went on to inform Monsieur the Mayor, who lived near the little square where nothing ever happened.

Pierre turned when they had left and entered my garden. What was he going to tell me now? I wondered, with sudden apprehension. Was I to serve another night?

"I'll be hanged if I will," I muttered.

He approached solemnly and slowly, his bayonet gleaming at his side, the warm sunlight glinting on the buttons of his uniform. When he got near enough for me to look into his eyes he stopped, raised his hand to his cap in salute, and said with a smile:

"Now, monsieur, the artichokes."

CHAPTER FIVE

MARIANNE

MONSIEUR LE CURÉ slid the long chair up to my fire, bent his straight, black body forward, and rubbing his chilled hands briskly before the blazing logs, announced with a smile of content:

"Marianne is out of jail."

"*Sacristi!*" I exclaimed, "and in mid-winter! It must be cold enough in that hut of hers by the marsh — poor old girl."

"And not a sou to be earned fishing," added the curé.

"Tell me about this last crime of hers," I asked.

Monsieur le Curé's face grew serious, then again the smile of content spread to the corners of his firm mouth.

"Oh! Nothing very gruesome," he confessed, then after a moment's silence he continued slowly: "Her children needed shoes
and warm things for the winter. Marianne stole
sixty *mètres* of nets from the fishing crew at
'The Three Wolves' — she is hopeless, my
friend." With a vibrant gesture he straightened
up in his chair and flashed his keen eyes to mine.
"For ten years I have tried to reform her," he
declared. "Bah!" — and he tossed the stump
of his cigarette into the blaze.

"You nursed her once through the small-
pox," said I, "when no one dared go near her.
The mayor told me so. I should think *that*
would have long ago persuaded her to do something for you in return."

"We go where we are needed," he replied
simply. "She will promise me nothing. One
might as well try to make a faithful parishioner
of a gipsy as to change Marianne for the better."
He brought his fist down sharply on the broad
arm of his chair. "I tell you," he went on
tensely, "Marianne is a woman of no morals
and no religion — a woman who allows no one

to dictate to her save a gendarme with a warrant
of arrest.   Hardly a winter passes but she goes
to jail.   She is a confirmed thief, a bad subject,"
he went on vibrantly.   "She can drink as no
three sailors can drink — and yet you know as
well as I do," he added, lowering his voice,
"that there is not a mother in Pont du Sable
who is as good to her children as Marianne."

"They are a brave little brood," I replied.
"I have heard that the eldest boy and girl
Marianne adopted, yet they resemble their
mother, with their fair curly hair and blue eyes,
as much as do the youngest boys and the little
girl."

"Marianne has had many lovers," returned the
curé gravely.   "There is not one of that brood
of hers that has yet been baptized."   An expression of pain crossed his face.   "I have tried
hard; Marianne is impossible."

"Yet you admit she has her qualities."

"Yes, good qualities," he confessed, filling a
fresh cigarette paper full of tobacco.   "Good
qualities," he reiterated.   "She has brought
up her children to be honest and she keeps them

clean. She has never stolen from her own village — it is a point of honour with her. Ah! you do not know Marianne as I know her."

"It seems to me you are growing enthusiastic over our worst vagabond," I laughed.

"I am," replied the curé frankly. "I believe in her; she is afraid of nothing. You see her as a vagabond — an outcast, and the next instant, *Parbleu!* she forces out of you your camaraderie — even your respect. You shake her by the hand, that straight old hag with her clear blue eyes, her square jaw and her hard face! She who walks with the stride of a man, who is as supple and strong as a sailor, and who looks you squarely in the eye and studies you calmly, at times disdainfully — even when drunk."

It was late when Monsieur le Curé left me alone by my fire. I cannot say "alone," for the Essence of Selfishness, was purring on my chest.

In this old *normand* house of mine by the marsh, there comes a silence at this hour which

is exhilarating.   Out of these winter midnights
come strange sounds, whirring flights of sea-
fowl whistle over my roof, in late for a lodging
on the marsh.   A heavy peasant's cart goes by,
groaning in agony under the brake.   When the
wind is from the sea, it is like a bevy of witches
shrilling my doom down the chimney.   "Aye,
aye, 'tis he," they seem to scream, "the stranger
— the s-t-r-a-n-g-e-r."   One's mind is alert
at this hour — one must be brave in a foreign
land.

And so I sat up late, smoking a black pipe that
gurgled in unison with the purring on my chest
while I thought seriously of Marianne.

I had seen her go laughing to jail two months
ago, handcuffed to a gendarme on the back seat
of the last car of the toy train.   It was an
occasion when every one in the lost village came
charitably out to have a look.   I remembered,
too, she sat there as garrulous as if she were
starting on a holiday — a few of her old cronies
crowded about her.   One by one, her children
gave their mother a parting hug — there were
no tears — and the gendarme sat beside her

with a stolid dignity befitting his duty to the
République. Then the whistle tooted twice —
a coughing puff of steam in the crisp sunlight,
a wheeze of wheels, and the toy train rumbled
slowly out of the village with its prisoner.
Marianne nodded and laughed back at the
waving group.

"*Bon voyage!*" croaked a little old woman,
lifting her claw. She had borrowed five francs
from the prisoner.

"*Au revoir!*" laughed back Marianne, but
the words were faint, for the last car was snaking
around the bend.

Thus Marianne went to jail. Now that she
is back, she takes her return as carelessly and
unblushingly as a *demi-mondaine* does her
annual return from Dinard.

When Marianne was eighteen, they tell me,
she was the prettiest girl in Pont du Sable, that
is to say, she was prettier than Emilienne Dagèt
at Bar la Rose, or than Berthe Pavoisiér, the
daughter of the miller at Tocqueville, who is
now in Paris. At eighteen, Marianne was slim
and blonde; moreover, she was as bold as a

hawk, and smiled as easily as she lied. At
twenty, she was rated as a valuable member of
any fishing crew that put out from the coast, for
they found her capable during a catch, and
steady in danger, always doing her share and a
little more for those who could not help themselves. She is still doing it, for in her stone hut
on the edge of the marsh that serves as shelter
for her children and her rough old self, she has
been charitable and given a winter's lodging
to three old wrecks of the sea. There are no
beds, but there are bunks filled with marsh-hay;
there is no furniture, but there are a few pots
and pans, and in one corner of the dirt floor, a
crackling fire of drift wood, and nearly always
enough applejack for all, and now and then hot
soup. Marianne wrenches these luxuries, so to
speak, out of the sea, often alone and single-
handed, working as hard as a gull to feed her
young.

The curé was right; Marianne had her good
qualities — I was almost beginning to wonder
to myself as I pulled drowsily at the black pipe
if her good qualities did not outweigh her bad

ones, when the Essence of Selfishness awakened
and yawned. And so it was high time to send
this spoiled child of mine to bed.

Marianne called her "*ma belle petite*," though
her real name was Yvonne — Yvonne Louise
Tournéveau.

Yvonne kept her black eyes from early dawn
until dark upon a dozen of the Père Bourron's
cows in her charge, who grazed on a long point
of the marsh, lush with salt grass, that lay sheltered back of the dunes fronting the open sea.

Now and then, when a cow strayed over the
dunes on to the hard beach beyond to gaze
stupidly at the breakers, the little girl's voice
would become as authoritative as a boy's. "*Eh
ben, tu sais!*" she would shout as she ran to head
the straggler off, adding some sound whacks
with a stick until the cow decided to lumber
back to the rest. "*Ah mais!*" Yvonne would
sigh as she seated herself again in the wire-grass,
tucking her firm bronzed legs under a patched
skirt that had once served as a winter petticoat
for the Mère Bourron.

Occasionally a trudging coast guard or a
lone hunter in passing would call "*Bonjour!*" to
her, and since she was pretty, this child of fifteen,
they would sometimes hail her with "*Ça va,
ma petite!*" and Yvonne would flush and reply
bravely, "*Mais oui, M'sieur, merci.*"

Since she was only a little girl with hair as
black as a gipsy's, a ruddy olive skin, fresh
young lips and a well-knit, compact body, hard-
ened by constant exposure to the sea air and sun,
no one bothered their heads much about her
name.   She was only a child who smiled when
the passerby would give her a chance, which
was seldom, and when she did, she disclosed
teeth as white as the tiny shells on the beach.
There were whole days on the marsh when she
saw no one.

At noon, when the cracked bell in the distant
belfry of the gray church of Pont du Sable sent
its discordant note quavering across the marsh,
Yvonne drew forth a sailor's knife from where
it lay tucked safe within the breast of her coarse
chemise, and untying a square of blue cotton
cloth, cut in two her portion of peasant

bread, saving half the bread and half a bottle
of Père Bourron's thinnest cider for the late
afternoon.

There were days, too, when Marianne coming up from the sea with her nets, stopped to
rest beside the child and talk. Yvonne having
no mother which she could remember, Marianne
had become a sort of transient mother to her,
whom the incoming tide sometimes brought her
and whom she would wait for with uncertain
expectancy, often for days.

One afternoon, early in the spring, when the
cows were feeding in the scant slanting shade
of the dunes, Yvonne fell asleep. She lay out
straight upon her back, her brown legs crossed,
one wrist over her eyes. She slept so soundly that
neither the breeze that had sprung up from the
northeast, stirring with every fresh puff the stray
locks about her small ears, or the sharp barking
of a dog hunting rabbits for himself over the
dunes, awakened her. Suddenly she became
conscious of being grasped in a pair of strong
arms, and, awakening with a little scream,
looked up into the grinning face of Marianne,

who straightway gave her a big, motherly hug
until she was quite awake and then kissed her
soundly on both cheeks, until Yvonne laughed
over her fright.

"*Oh, mon Dieu!* but I was frightened,"
sighed the child, and sat up straight, smoothing
back her tumbled hair. "Oh! la! la!" she
gasped.

"They are beauties, *hein!*" exclaimed Marianne, nodding to an oozing basketful of mackerel;
then, kneeling by the basket, she plunged her
red hands under the slimy, glittering mass of
fish, lifting and dropping them that the child
might see the average size in the catch.

"*Eh ben!*" declared Marianne, "some day
when thou art bigger, *ma petite*, I'll take thee
where thou canst make some silver. There's
half a louis' worth there if there's a sou!" There
was a gleam of satisfaction in her eyes, as she
bent over her basket again, dressed as she was
in a pair of fisherman's trousers cut off at the
knees.

"One can play the lady on half a louis," she
continued, covering her fish from the sun with

her bundle of nets. "My man shall have a full bottle of the best to-night," she added, wiping her wet hands across her strong bare knees.

"How much 'cake' does that old crab of a Bourron pay thee?" she inquired, turning again to the child.

"Six sous a day, and then my food and lodging," confessed Yvonne.

"He won't ruin himself," muttered Marianne.

"They say the girl at the Three Wolves gets ten," added the child with awe, "but thou knowest how — she must do the washing besides."

Marianne's square jaw shut hard. She glanced at Yvonne's patched skirt, the one that had been the Mère Bourron's winter petticoat, feeling its quality as critically as a fashionable dressmaker.

"*Sacristi!*" she exclaimed, examining a rent, "there's one door that the little north wind won't knock twice at before he enters. Keep still, *ma petite*, I've got thread and a needle."

She drew from her trousers' pocket a leather wallet in which lay four two-sous pieces, an iron key and a sail needle driven through a ball of linen thread. "It is easily seen thou art not in love," laughed Marianne, as she cross-stitched the tear. "Thou wilt pay ten sous for a ribbon gladly some day when thou art in love."

The child was silent while she sewed. Presently she asked timidly, "One eats well there?"

"Where?"

"But thou knowest — *there.*"

"In the prison?"

"*Mais oui,*" whispered Yvonne.

"Of course," growled Marianne, "one eats well; it is perfect. *Tiens!* we have the good soup, that is well understood; and now and then meat and rice."

"Oh!" exclaimed the child in awe.

"*Mais oui,*" assured Marianne with a nod, "and prunes."

"Where is that, the prison?" ventured the child.

"It is very far," returned Marianne, biting

off the thread, "and it is not for every one
either," she added with a touch of pride — "only
I happen to be an old friend and know the
judge."

"And how much does it cost a day, the
prison?" asked Yvonne.

"Not *that*," replied Marianne, snipping her
single front tooth knowingly with the tip of her
nail.

"*Mon Dieu!* and they give you all that for
nothing?" exclaimed the child in astonishment.
"It is *chic*, that, *hein!*" and she nodded her
pretty head with decision, "*Ah mais oui, alors!*"
she laughed.

"I must be going," said Marianne, abruptly.
"My young ones will be wanting their soup."
She flattened her back against her heavy basket,
slipped the straps under her armpits and rose
to her feet, the child passing the bundle of nets
to her and helping her shoulder them to the
proper balance.

"*Au revoir, ma belle petite*," she said, bending to kiss the girl's cheek; then with her free
hand she dove into her trousers' pocket and

drew out a two-sous piece. "*Tiens,*" she exclaimed, pressing the copper into the child's hand.

Yvonne gave a little sigh of delight. It was not often she had two sous all to herself to do what she pleased with, which doubles the delight of possession. Besides, the Mère Bourron kept her wages — or rather, count of them, which was cheaper — on the back page of a greasy book wherein were registered the births of calves.

"*Au revoir,*" reiterated Marianne, and turned on her way to the village down the trail that wound through the salt grass out to the road skirting the bay. Yvonne watched her until she finally disappeared through a cut in the dunes that led to the main road.

The marsh lay in the twilight, the curlews were passing overhead bound for a distant mud flat for the night. "*Courli! Courli!*" they called, the old birds with a rasp, the young ones cheerfully; as one says "*bonsoir.*" The cows, conscious of the fast-approaching dark, were moving toward the child. She stood still until they had passed her, then drove them slowly back to the Père Bourron's, her two-sous piece clutched safe in her hand.

It was dark when she let down the bars of the orchard, leading into the farm-yard. Here the air was moist and heavy with the pungent odour of manure; a turkey gobbler and four timid hens roosting in a low apple tree, stirred uneasily as the cows passed beneath them to their stable next to the kitchen — a stable with a long stone manger and walls two feet thick. Above the stable was a loft covered by a thatched roof; it was in a corner of this loft, in a large box filled with straw and provided with a patchwork-quilt, that Yvonne slept.

A light from the kitchen window streamed across the muddy court. The Père and Mère Bourron were already at supper. The child bolted the stable door upon her herd and slipped into her place at table with a timid "*Bonsoir, m'sieur, madame*," to her masters, which was acknowledged by a grunt from the Père Bourron and a spasm of coughing from his spouse.

The Mère Bourron, who had the dullish round

eye of a pig that gleamed suspiciously when
she became inquisitive, had supped well.   Now
and then she squinted over her fat jowls veined
with purple, plying her mate with short, savage
questions, for he had sold cattle that day at the
market at Bonville.   Such evenings as these
were always quarrelsome between the two, and
as the little girl did not count any more than the
chair she sat in, they argued openly over the
day's sale.   The best steer had brought less
than the Mère Bourron had believed, a shrewd
possibility, even after a month's bargaining.
When both had wiped their plates clean with
bread — for nothing went to waste there — the
child got up and brought the black coffee and
the decanter of applejack.   They at last ceased
to argue, since the Mère Bourron had had the
final word.   Père Bourron sat with closed fists,
opening one now and then to strengthen his
coffee with applejack.   Being a short, thick-
set man, he generally sat in his blouse after he
had eaten, with his elbows on the table and his
rough bullet-like head, with its crop of unkempt
hair, buried in his hands.

When Yvonne had finished her soup, and eaten all her bread, she rose and with another timid "*Bonsoir*" slipped away to bed.

"Leave the brindle heifer tied!" shrilled madame as the child reached the courtyard.

"*Mais, oui madame*, it is done," answered Yvonne, and crept into her box beneath the thatch.

At sixteen Yvonne was still guarding the cows for the Bourrons. At seventeen she fell in love.

He was a slick, slim youth named Jean, with a soapy blond lock plastered under the visor of his leather cap pulled down to his red ears. On fête days, he wore in addition a scarlet necktie girdling his scrawny throat. He had watched Yvonne for a long time, very much as the snake in the fable saved the young dove until it was grown.

And so, Yvonne grew to dreaming while the cows strayed. Once the Père Bourron struck at her with a spade for her negligence, but missed. Another night he beat her soundly for letting

a cow get stalled in the mud.   The days on the
marsh now became interminable, for he worked
for Gavelle, the carpenter, a good three *kilo-
mètres* back of Pont du Sable and the two could
see each other only on fête days when he met
her secretly among the dunes or in the evenings
near the farm.   He would wait for her then at
the edge of the woods skirting the misty sea of
pasture that spread out below the farm like
some vast and silent dry lake, dotted here and
there with groups of sleeping cattle.

She saw Marianne but seldom now, for the
latter fished mostly at the Three Wolves, sharing
her catch with a crew of eight fishermen.   Often
they would seine the edge of the coast, their
boat dancing off beyond the breakers while
they netted the shallow water, swishing up the
hard beach — these gamblers of the sea.   They
worked with skill and precision, each one having
his share to do, while one — the quickest —
was appointed to carry their bundle of dry
clothes rolled in a tarpaulin.

Marianne seemed of casual importance to
her now.   We seldom think of our best friends

in time of love. Yvonne cried for his kisses
which at first she did not wholly understand,
but which she grew to hunger for, just as when
she was little she craved for all she wanted to
eat for once — and candy.

She began to think of herself, too — of Jean's
scarlet cravat — of his new shoes too tight for
him, which he wore with the pride of a village
dandy on fête days and Sundays — and of her
own patched and pitifully scanty wardrobe.

"She has nothing, that little one," she had
heard the gossips remark openly before her,
time and time again, when she was a child.
Now that she was budding into womanhood
and was physically twice as strong as Jean,
now that she was conscious of *herself*, she began
to know the pangs of vanity.

It was about this time that she bought the
ribbon, just as Marianne had foretold, a red
ribbon to match Jean's tie, and which she fashioned into a bow and kept in a paper box, well
hidden in the straw of her bed. The patched
skirt had long ago grown too short, and was now
stuffed into a broken window beyond the cow

manger to temper the draught from the neck
of a sick bull.

She wore now, when it stormed, thick woollen
stockings and sabots; and another skirt of the
Mère Bourron's fastened around a chemise of
coarse homespun linen, its colour faded to
a delicious pale mazarine blue, showing the
strength and fullness of her body.

She had stolen down from the loft this night
to meet him at the edge of the woods.

"Where is he?" were his first words as he
sought her lips in the dark.

"He has gone," she whispered, when her lips
were free.

"Where?"

"*Eh ben*, he went away with the Père Detour
to the village — madame is asleep."

"Ah, good!" said he.

"*Mon Dieu!* but you are warm," she whispered, pressing her cheek against his own.

"I ran," he drawled, "the patron kept me
late. There is plenty of work there now."

He put his arm around her and the two

walked deeper into the wood, he holding her
heavy moist hand idly in his own. Presently
the moon came out, sailing high among the
scudding clouds, flashing bright in the clear
intervals. A white mist had settled low over
the pasture below them, and the cattle were
beginning to move restlessly under the chill
blanket, changing again and again their places
for the night. A bull bellowed with all his
might from beyond the mysterious distance.
He had evidently scented them, for presently
he emerged from the mist and moved along
the edge of the woods, protected by a deep
ditch. He stopped when he was abreast of
them to bellow again, then kept slowly on past
them. They had seated themselves in the moonlight among the stumps of some freshly cut
poplars.

"*Dis donc*, what is the matter?" he asked
at length, noticing her unusual silence, for she
generally prattled on, telling him of the unevent-
ful hours of her days.

"Nothing," she returned evasively.

"*Mais si; bon Dieu!* there *is* something."

She placed her hands on her trembling knees.

"No, I swear there is nothing, Jean," she said faintly.

But he insisted.

"One earns so little," she confessed at length. "Ten sous a day, it is not much, and the days are so long on the marsh. If I knew how to cook I'd try and get a place like Emilienne."

"Bah!" said he, "you are crazy — one must study to cook; besides, you are not yet eighteen, the Père Bourron has yet the right to you for a year."

"That is true," confessed the girl simply; "one has not much chance when one is an orphan. Listen, Jean."

"What?"

"Listen — is it true that thou dost love me?"

"Surely," he replied with an easy laugh.

"Listen," she repeated timidly; "if thou shouldst get steady work — I should be content . . . to be . . . " But her voice became inaudible.

"*Allons!* . . . what?" he demanded irritably.

"To . . . to be married," she whispered.

He started. "*Eh ben! en voilà* an idea!" he exclaimed.

"Forgive me, Jean, I have always had that idea ——" She dried her eyes on the back of her hand and tried hard to smile. "It is foolish, eh? The marriage costs so dear . . . but if thou shouldst get steady work . . ."

"*Eh ben!*" he answered slowly with his Normand shrewdness, "I don't say no."

"I'll help thee, Jean; I can work hard when I am free. One wins forty sous a day by washing, and then there is the harvest."

There was a certain stubborn conviction in her words which worried him.

"*Eh ben!*" he said at length, "we might get married — that's so."

She caught her breath.

"Swear it, Jean, that thou wilt marry me, swear it upon Sainte Marie."

"*Eh voilà*, it's done. *Oui*, by Sainte Marie!"

She threw her arms about him, crushing him against her breast.

"*Dieu!* but thou art strong," he whispered.

"Did I hurt thee?"

"No — thou art content now?"

"Yes — I am content," she sobbed, "I am content, I am content."

He had slipped to the ground beside her. She drew his head back in her lap, her hand pressed hard against his forehead.

"*Dieu!* but I am content," she breathed in his ear.

He felt her warm tears dropping fast upon his cheek.

All night she lay in the straw wide awake, flushed, in a sort of fever. At daylight she drove her cows back to the marsh without having barely touched her soup.

Far across the bay glistened the roof of a barn under construction. An object the size of a beetle was crawling over the new boards.

It was Jean.

"I'm a fool," he thought, as he drove in a nail. Then he fell to thinking of a girl in his own village whose father was as rich as the Père Bourron.

"*Sacré Diable!*" he laughed at length, "if every one got married who had sworn by Sainte Marie, Monsieur le Curé would do a good business."

A month later Père Bourron sold out a cartful of calves at the market at Bonville. It was late at night when he closed his last bargain over a final glass, climbed up on his big two-wheeled cart, and with a face of dull crimson and a glazed eye, gathered up the reins and started swaying in his seat for home. A boy carrying milk found him at daylight the next morning lying face down in the track of his cart, dead, with a fractured skull. Before another month had passed, the Mère Bourron had sold the farm and gone to live with her sister — a lean woman who took in sewing.

Yvonne was free.

Free to work and to be married, and she did work with silent ferocity from dawn until dark, washing the heavy coarse linen for a farm, and scrubbing the milk-pans bright until often long after midnight — and saved. Jean worked too, but mostly when he pleased, and had his hair cut on fête days, most of which he spent in the café and saw Yvonne during the odd moments when she was free.

Life over the blacksmith's shop, where she had taken a room, went merrily for a while. Six months later — it is such an old story that it is hardly worth the telling — but it was long after dark when she got back from work and she found it lying on the table in her rough clean little room — a scrap of paper beside some tiny worsted things she had been knitting for weeks.

"I am not coming back," she read in an illiterate hand.

She would have screamed, but she could not breathe. She turned again, staring at the paper and gripping the edge of the table with both hands — then the ugly little room that smelt of singed hoofs rocked and swam before her.

When she awoke she lay on the floor. The flame of the candle was sputtering in its socket. After a while she crawled to her knees in the dark; then, somehow, she got to her feet and groped her way to the door, and down the narrow stairs out to the road. She felt the need of a mother and turned toward Pont du Sable, keeping to the path at the side of the wood like a homeless dog, not wishing to be observed. Every little while, she was seized with violent trembling so that she was obliged to stop — her whole body ached as if she had been beaten.

A sharp wind was whistling in from the sea and the night was so black that the road bed was barely visible.

It was some time before she reached the beginning of Pont du Sable, and turned down a forgotten path that ran back of the village by the marsh. A light gleamed ahead — the lantern of a fishing-boat moored far out on the slimy mud. She pushed on toward it, mistaking its position, in her agony, for the hut of Marianne. Before she knew it, she was well out on the treacherous mud, slipping and sinking. She had no longer the strength now to pull her tired feet out. Twice she sank in the slime above her knees. She tried to go back but

the mud had become ooze — she was sinking —
she screamed — she was gone and she knew it.
Then she slipped and fell on her face in a glaze
of water from the incoming tide. At this
instant some one shouted back, but she did not
hear.

It was Marianne.

It was she who had moored the boat with the
lantern and was on her way back to her hut
when she heard a woman scream twice. She
stopped as suddenly as if she had been shot at,
straining her eyes in the direction the sound
came from — she knew that there was no worse
spot in the bay, a semi-floating solution of mud
veined with quicksand. She knew, too, how
far the incoming tide had reached, for she had
just left it at her bare heels by way of a winding
narrow causeway with a hard shell bottom that
led to the marsh. She did not call for help, for
she knew what lay before her and there was not
a second to lose. The next instant, she had
sprung out on the treacherous slime, running
for a life in the fast-deepening glaze of water.

"Lie down!" she shouted. Then her feet

touched a solid spot caked with shell and grass. Here she halted for an instant to listen — a choking groan caught her ear.

"Lie down!" she shouted again and sprang forward. She knew the knack of running on that treacherous slime.

She leapt to a patch of shell and listened again. The woman was choking not ten yards ahead of her, almost within reach of a thin point of matted grass running back of the marsh, and there she found her, and she was still breathing. With her great strength she slid her to the point of grass. It held them both. Then she lifted her bodily in her arms, swung her on her back and ran splashing knee-deep in water to solid ground.

"*Sacré bon Dieu!*" she sobbed as she staggered with her burden. "*C'est ma belle petite!*"

For weeks Yvonne lay in the hut of the worst vagabond of Pont du Sable. So did a mite of humanity with black eyes who cried and laughed when he pleased. And Marianne fished for them both, alone and single-handed, wrenching

time and time again comforts from the sea, for
she would allow no one to go near them, not
even such old friends as Monsieur le Curé and
myself — that old hag, with her clear blue eyes,
who walks with the stride of a man, and who
looks at you squarely, at times disdainfully —
even when drunk.

CHAPTER SIX

THE BARON'S PERFECTOS

STRANGE things happen in my "Village of Vagabonds." It is not all fisher girls, Bohemian neighbours, romance, and that good friend the curé who shoots one day and confesses sinners the next. Things from the outside world come to us — happenings with sometimes a note of terror in them to make one remember their details for days.

Only the other day I had run up from the sea to Paris to replenish the larder of my house abandoned by the marsh at Pont du Sable, and was sitting behind a glass of vermouth on the terrace of the Café de la Paix when the curtain rose.

One has a desire to promenade with no

definite purpose these soft spring days, when all Paris glitters in the warm sun. The days slip by, one into another — days to be lazy in, idle and extravagant, to promenade alone, seeking adventure, and thus win a memory, if only the amiable glance of a woman's eyes.

I was drinking in the tender air, when from my seat on the terrace I recognized in the passing throng the familiar figure of the Brazilian banker, the Baron Santos da Granja. The caress of spring had enticed the Baron early this afternoon to the Boulevard. Although he had been pointed out to me but once, there was no mistaking his conspicuous figure as he strode on through the current of humanity, for he stood head and shoulders above the average mortal, and many turned to glance at this swarthy, alert, well-preserved man of the world with his keen black eyes, thin pointed beard and moustache of iron gray. From his patent-leather boots to his glistening silk hat the Baron Santos da Granja was immaculate.

Suddenly I saw him stop, run his eyes swiftly over the crowded tables and then, though there happened to be one just vacated within his reach, turn back with a look of decision and enter the Government's dépôt for tobacco under the Grand Hotel.

I, too, was in need of tobacco, for had not my good little maid-of-all-work, Suzette, announced to me only the day before:

"Monsieur, there are but three left of the big cigars in the thin box; and the ham of the English that monsieur purchased in Paris is no more."

"It is well, my child," I had returned resignedly, "that ham could not last forever; it was too good."

"And if Monsieur le Curé comes to dinner there is no more kümmel," the little maid had confessed, and added with a shy lifting of her truthful eyes, "monsieur does not wish I should get more of the black cigars at the grocery?"

I had winced as I recalled the last box, purchased from the only store in Pont du Sable, where they had lain long enough to absorb the pungent odour of dried herring and kerosene.

Of course it was not right that our guests
should suffer thus from an empty larder and so,
as I have said, I had run up from the sea to
replenish it. It was, I confess, an extravagant
way of doing one's marketing; but then
there was Paris in the spring beckoning me,
and who can resist her seductive call at such a
time?

But to my story: I finished my glass of
vermouth, and, following the Baron's example,
entered the Government's store, where I discovered him selecting with the air of a connois-
seur a dozen thin boxes of rare perfectos. He
chatted pleasantly with the clerk who served
him and upon going to the desk, opened a
Russian-leather portfolio and laid before the
cashier six crisp, new one-hundred-franc notes
in payment for the lot. I have said that the
Baron was immaculate, and he *was*, even to
his money. It was as spotless and unruffled as
his linen, as neat, in fact, as were the noble
perfectos of his choice, long, mild and pure,
with tiny ends, and fat, comforting bodies
that guaranteed a quality fit for an emperor;

but then the least a bank can do, I imagine, is to provide clean money to its president.

As the Baron passed out and my own turn at the desk came to settle for my modest provision of Havanas, I recalled to my mind the current gossip of the Baron's extravagance, of the dinners he had lately given that surprised Paris — and Paris is not easily surprised. What if he had "sold more than half of his vast estate in Brazil last year"? And suppose he was no longer able or willing "to personally supervise his racing stable," that he "had grown tired of the track," etc. Nonsense! The press knows so little of the real truth. For me the Baron Santos da Granja was simply a seasoned man of the world, with the good taste to have retired from its conspicuous notoriety; and good taste is always expensive. His bank account did not interest me.

I knew her well by sight, for she passed me often in the Bois de Boulogne when I ran up to Paris on just such errands as my present one. She had given me thus now and then glimpses

of her feverish life — gleams from the facets,
since her success in Paris was as brilliant as a
diamond. Occasionally I would meet her in
the shaded alleys, but always in sight of her
brougham, which kept pace with her whims at
a safe but discreet distance.

There was a rare perfection about her lithe,
graceful person, an ease and subtlety of line, an
allure which was satisfying — from her trim
little feet gloved in suède, to the slender nape of
her neck, from which sprang, back of the love-
liest of little ears, the exquisite sheen of her
blonde hair.

There were mornings when she wore a
faultless tailor-made of plain dark blue and
carried a scarlet parasol, with its jewelled
handle held in a firm little hand secreted in
spotless white kid.

I noticed, too, in passing that her eyes were
deep violet and exceedingly alert, her features
classic in their fineness. Once I saw her smile,
not at me, but at her fox terrier. It was then
that I caught a glimpse of her young white teeth
— pearly white in contrast to the freshness of

her pink and olive skin, so clear that it seemed to be translucent, and she blushed easily, having lived but a score of springs all told.

In the afternoon, when she drove in her brougham lined with dove-gray, the scarlet parasol was substituted by one of filmy, creamy lace, shading a gown of pale mauve or champagne colour.

I had heard that she was passionately extravagant, that she seldom, if ever, won at the races — owned a little hotel with a carved façade in the Avenue du Bois, a villa at Dinard, and three fluffy little dogs, who jingled their gold bells when they followed her.

She dined at Paillard's, sometimes at the Café de la Paix, rarely at Maxim's; skated at the Palais de Glace on the most respectable afternoons — drank plain water — rolled her own cigarettes — and possessed a small jewel box full of emeralds, which she seldom wore.

Voilà! A spoiled child for you!

There were mornings, too, when, after her tub, as early as nine, she galloped away on her cob,

to the *Bois* for her coffee and hot *brioche* at the
Pré Catelan, a romantic little farm with a café
and a stableful of mild-eyed cows that provide
fresh milk to the weary at daylight, who are
trying hard to turn over a new leaf before the
next midnight. Often she came there accom-
panied by her groom and the three little dogs
with the jingling bells, who enjoyed the warm
milk and the run back of the fleet hoofs of her
saddle-horse.

On this very morning — upon which opens
the second act of my drama, I found her sitting
at the next table to mine, chiding one of the
jingling little dogs for his disobedience.

"*Eh ben! tu sais!*" she exclaimed suddenly,
with a savage gleam in her eyes.

I turned and gazed at her in astonishment.
It was the first time I had heard her voice. It
was her accent that made me stare.

"*Eh ben! tu sais!*" she repeated, in the
patois of the Normand peasant, lifting her
riding crop in warning to the ball of fluff who
had refused to get on his chair and was now
wriggling in apology.

"Who is that lady?" I asked the old waiter Emile, who was serving me.

"Madame is an Austrian," he confided to me, bending his fat back as he poured my coffee.

"Austrian, eh! Are you certain, Emile?"

"*Parbleu*, monsieur" replied Emile, "one is never certain of any one in Paris. I only tell monsieur what I have heard. Ah! it is very easy to be mistaken in Paris, monsieur. Take, for instance, the lady in deep mourning, with the two little girls, over there at the table under the lilac bush."

"She is young to be a widow," I interposed, glancing discreetly in the direction he nodded.

Emile smiled faintly. "She is not a widow, monsieur," he returned, "neither is she as Spanish as she looks; she is Polish and dances at the Folies Parisiennes under the name of *La Belle Gueritta* from Seville."

"But her children look French," I ventured.

"They are the two little girls of her concierge, monsieur." Emile's smile widened until it spread in merry wrinkles to the corners of his twinkling eyes.

"In all that lace and velvet?" I exclaimed.

"Precisely, monsieur."

"And why the deep mourning, Emile?"

"It is a pose, monsieur. One must invent novelties, eh? when one is as good-looking as that. Besides, madame's reputation has not been of the best for some time. Monsieur possibly remembers the little affair last year in the Rue des Mathurins? Very well, it was she who extracted the hundred thousand francs from the Marquis de Villiers. Madame now gives largely to charity and goes to mass."

"Blackmail, Emile?"

"Of the worst kind, and so monsieur sees how easily one can be mistaken, is it not so? *Sacristi!* one never knows."

"But are you certain you are not mistaken about your Austrian, Emile?" I ventured.

He shrugged his shoulders as if in apology for his opinion, and I turned again to study his Austrian. The noses of her little dogs with the jingling bells were now contentedly immersed in a bowl of milk.

A moment later I saw her lift her clear

violet eyes and catch sight of one of the milkers,
who was trying to lead a balky cow through
the court by a rope badly knotted over her
horns. She was smiling as she sat watching
the cow, who now refused to budge. The boy
was losing his temper when she broke into a
rippling laugh, rose, and going over to the unruly
beast, unknotted the rope from her horns and,
replacing it by two half hitches with the ease
and skill of a sailor, handed the rope back to
the boy.

"There, you little stupid!" she exclaimed,
"she will lead better now. *Allez!*" she cried,
giving the cow a sharp rap on her rump. "*Allez!
Hup!*"

A murmur of surprise escaped Emile. "It
is not the first time madame has done that
trick," he remarked under his hand, as she
crossed the courtyard to regain her chair.

"She is Normande," I declared, "I am certain
of it by the way she said '*Eh ben!*' And did
you not notice her walk back to her table?
Erect, with the easy, quick step of a fisher girl?
The same walk of the race of fisher girls who

live in my village," I continued with enthusiastic decision. "There is no mistaking it; it is peculiar to Pont du Sable, and note, too, her *patois!*"

"It is quite possible, monsieur," replied Emile, "but it does not surprise me. One sees every one in Paris. There are few *grandes dames* left. When one has been a *garçon de café*, as I have, for over thirty years, one is surprised at nothing; not even —— "

The tap of a gold coin on the rim of a cold saucer interrupted our talk. The summons was from my lady who had conquered the cow.

"*Voilà*, madame!" cried Emile, as he left me to hasten to her table, where he made the change, slipped the *pourboire* she gave him into his alpaca pocket, and with a respectful, "*Merci bien*, madame," drew back her chair as she rose and summoned her groom, who a moment later stood ready to help her mount. The next instant I saw her hastily withdraw her small foot from the hollow of his coarse hand, and wave to a passing horse and rider. The rider, whose features were half hidden

under the turned-down brim of a panama,
wheeled his horse, reined up before her, dismounted, threw his rein to her groom and
bending, kissed her on both cheeks. She laughed;
murmured something in his ear; the panama
nodded in reply, then, slipping his arm under
her own, the two entered the courtyard. There
they were greeted by Emile.

"Madame and I will breakfast here to-day,
Emile," said the voice beneath the panama.
"The little table in the corner and the same
Pommard."

He threw his riding crop on a vacant chair and,
lifting his hat, handed it to the veteran waiter.

It was the Baron Santos da Granja!

Hidden at the foot of a plateau skirting the
desert marshes, two miles above my village of
Pont du Sable, lies in ruins all that remains of
the deserted village known as La Poche.

It is well named "The Pocket," since for
years it served as a safe receptacle for itinerant
beggars and fugitives from justice who found
an ideal retreat among its limestone quarries,

which, being long abandoned, provided holes in the steep hillside for certain vagabonds, who paid neither taxes to the government, nor heed to its law.

There is an old cattle trail that leads to La Poche, crossed now and then by overgrown paths, that wind up through a labyrinth of briers, rank ferns and matted growth to the plateau spreading back from the hillside. I use this path often as a short cut home.

One evening I had shot late on the marshes and started for home by way of La Poche. It was bright moonlight when I reached a trail new to me and approached the deserted village by way of a tangled, overgrown road.

The wind had gone down with the rising of the moon, and the intense stillness of the place was such that I could hear about me in the tangle the lifting of a trampled weed and the moving of the insects as my boots disturbed them. The silence was uncanny. Under the brilliancy of the moon all things gleamed clear in a mystic light, their shadows as black as the sunken pits of a cave.

I pushed on through the matted growth, with the collar of my leather coat buttoned up, my cap pulled down, and my hands thrust in my sleeves, hugging my gun under my arm, for the briars made tough going.

Presently, I got free of the tangle and out to a grassy stretch of road, once part of the river bed. Here and there emerged, from the matted tangle of the hillside flanking it, the ruins of La Poche. Often only a single wall or a tottering chimney remained silhouetted against the skeleton of a gabled roof; its rafters stripped of tiles, gleaming in the moonlight like the ribs and breastbone of a carcass.

If La Poche is a place to be shunned by day — at night it becomes terrible; it seems to breathe the hidden viciousness of its past, as if its ruins were the tombs of its bygone criminals.

I kept on the road, passed another carcass and drew abreast of a third, which I stepped out of the road to examine. Both its floors had long before I was born dropped into its cellar; its threshold beneath my feet was slippery with green slime; I looked up through its ribs, from which hung festoons of cobwebs and dead vines, like shreds of dried flesh hanging from a skeleton.

Still pursuing my way, I came across an old well; the bucket was drawn up and its chain wet; it was the first sign of habitation I had come across. As my hand touched the windlass, I instinctively gave it a turn; it creaked dismally and a dog barked savagely at the sound from somewhere up the hillside; then the sharp, snappy yelping of other dogs higher up followed.

I stopped, felt in my pockets and slipped two shells into my gun, heavily loaded for duck, with the feeling that if I were forced to shoot I would hold high over their heads. As I closed the breech of my gun and clicked back my hammers to be ready for any emergency, the tall figure of a man loomed up in the grassy road ahead of me, his legs in a ray of moonlight, the rest of him in shadow.

"Does this road lead out to the main road?" I called to him, not being any too sure that it did.

"Who is there?" he demanded sharply

and in perfect French; then he advanced and
I saw that the heavy stick he carried with a
firm grip was mounted in silver.

"A hunter, monsieur," I returned pleasantly,
noticing now his dress and bearing.

It was so dark where we stood, that I could
not yet distinguish his features.

"May I ask you, monsieur, whom I have
the pleasure of meeting," I ventured, my mind
now more at rest.

He strode toward me.

"My name is de Brissac," said he, extending
his hand. "Forgive me," he added with a good-
natured laugh, "if I startled you; it is hardly
the place to meet a gentleman in at this hour.
Have you missed your way?"

"No," I replied, "I shot late and took a short
cut to reach my home." I pointed in the
direction of the marshes while I searched his face
which was still shrouded in gloom, in my effort
to see what manner of man I had run across.

"And have you had good luck?" he inquired
with a certain meaning in his voice, as if he
was still in doubt regarding my trespass.

"Not worth speaking of," I returned in as calm a voice as I could muster; "the birds are mostly gone. And do you shoot also, may I ask?"

"It is an incorrigible habit with me," he confessed in a more reassured tone. "I have, however, not done so badly of late with the birds; I killed seventeen plovers this morning— a fine lot."

Here his tone changed. All his former reserve had vanished. "Come with me," said he; "I insist; I'll show you what I killed; they make a pretty string, I assure you. You shall see, too, presently, my house; it is the one with the new roof. Do you happen to have seen it?"

This came with a certain note of seriousness in his voice.

"No. but I am certain it must be a luxury in the débris," I laughed; "but," I added, "I am afraid I must postpone the pleasure until another time." I was still undecided as to my course.

Again his tone changed to one of extreme courtesy, as if he had been quick to notice my hesitation.

"I know it is late," said he, "but I must insist on your accepting my hospitality. The main road lies at the end of the plateau, and I will see you safely out to it and on your way home."

I paused before answering. Under the circumstances, I knew, I could not very well refuse, and yet I had a certain dread of accepting too easily. In France such refusals are sometimes considered as insults. "Thank you," I said at last, resolved to see the adventure out; "I accept with pleasure," adding with a laugh and speaking to his shadowy bulk, for I could not yet see his face:

"What silent mystery, what an uncanny fascination this place has about it! Even our meeting seems part of it. Don't you think so?"

"Yes, there is a peculiar charm here," he replied, in a more cautious tone as he led me into a narrow trail, "a charm that has taken hold of me, so that I bury myself here occasionally; it is a rest from Paris."

From Paris, eh? I thought — then he does not belong to the coast.

I edged nearer, determined now to catch a

glimpse of his features, the light of the moon having grown stronger. As he turned, its rays illumined his face and at the same instant a curious gleam flashed into his eyes.

Again the Baron da Granja stood before me.

Da Granja! the rich Brazilian! President of one of the biggest foreign banks in Paris. Man of the world, with a string of horses famous for years on a dozen race tracks. What the devil was he doing here? Had the cares of his bank driven him to such a lonely hermitage as La Poche? It seemed incredible, and yet there was not the slightest doubt as to his identity — I had seen him too often to be mistaken. His voice, too, now came back to me.

He strode on, and for some minutes kept silent, then he stopped suddenly and in a voice in which the old doubting tones were again audible said:

"You are English?"

Here he barred the path.

"No," I answered, a little ill at ease at his sudden change of manner. "American, from New York."

"And yet, I think I have seen you in Paris," he replied, after a moment's hesitation, his eyes boring into mine, which the light of the moon now made clear to him.

"It is quite possible," I returned calmly; "I think I have seen you also, monsieur; I am often in Paris."

Again he looked at me searchingly.

"Where?" he asked.

"At the Government's store, buying cigars." I did not intend to go any further.

He smiled as if relieved. He had been either trying to place me, or his suspicions had been again aroused, I could not tell which. One thing was certain: he was convinced I had swallowed the name "de Brissac" easily.

All at once his genial manner returned. "This way, to the right," he exclaimed. "Pardon me if I lead the way; the path is winding. My ruin, as I sometimes call it, is only a little farther up, and you shall have a long whiskey and siphon when you get there. You know Pont du Sable, of course," he continued as I kept in his tracks; the talk having again turned on his love of sport.

"Somewhat. I live there."

This time the surprise was his.

"Is it possible?" he cried, laying his **hand on** my shoulder, his face alight.

"Yes, my house is the once-abandoned one with the wall down by the marsh."

"Ah!" he burst out, "so you are *the* American, the newcomer, the man I have heard so much about, the man who is always shooting; and how the devil, may I ask, did you come to settle in Pont du Sable?"

"Well, you see, every one said it was such a wretched hole that I felt there must be some good in it. I have found it charming, and with the shooting it has become an old friend. I am glad also to find that you like it well enough to (it was I who hesitated now) to visit it."

"Yes, to shoot is always a relief," he answered evasively, and then in a more determined voice added, "This way, to the right, over the rocks! Come, give me your gun! The stones are slippery."

"No, I will carry it," I replied. "I am used to carrying it," and though my voice did not

betray me, I proposed to continue to carry it.
It was at least a protection against a walking
stick with a silver top. My mind being still
occupied with his suspicions, his inquiries, and
most of all his persistence that I should visit
his house, with no other object in view than a
whiskey and siphon and a string of plovers.
And yet, despite the gruesomeness of the sur-
roundings, while alert as to his slightest move,
I was determined to see the adventure through.

He did not insist, but turned sharply to the
left, and the next instant I stood before the
threshold of a low stone house with a new tiled
roof. A squat, snug house, the eaves of whose
steep gabled roof came down well over its two
stories, like the snuffer on a candle. He stepped
to the threshold, felt about the door as if in
search for a latch, and rapped three times with
the flat of his hand. Then he called softly:

"Léa!"

"*C'est toi?*" came in answer, and a small
hand cautiously opened a heavy overhead
shutter, back of which a shaded lamp was
burning.

"Yes, it is all right, it is I," said he. "Come down! I have a surprise for you. I have captured an American."

There came the sound of tripping feet, the quick drawing of a heavy bolt, and the door opened.

My little lady of the Pré Catelan!

Not in a tea-gown from the Rue de la Paix — nothing of that kind whatever; not a ruffle, not a jewel — but clothed in the well-worn garment of a fisher girl of the coast — a coarse homespun chemise of linen, open at the throat, and a still coarser petticoat of blue, faded by the salt sea — a fisher girl's petticoat that stopped at her knees, showing her trim bare legs and the white insteps of her little feet, incased in a pair of heelless felt slippers.

For the second time I was treated to a surprise. Really, Pont du Sable was not so dead a village after all.

Emile was wrong. She was one of my village people.

My host did not notice my astonishment, but waved his hand courteously.

"*Entrez*, monsieur!" he cried with a laugh, and then, turning sharply, he closed the door and bolted it.

I looked about me.

We were in a rough little room, that would have won any hunter's heart; there were solid racks, heavy with guns, on the walls, a snapping wood fire, and a clean table, laid for dinner, and lastly, the chair quickly drawn to it for the waiting guest. This last they laughingly forced me into, for they both insisted I should dine with them — an invitation which I gladly accepted, for my fears were now completely allayed.

We talked of the neighbourbood, of hunting, of Paris, of the new play at the Nouveautés — I did not mention the Bois. One rarely mentions in France having seen a woman out of her own home, although I was sure she remembered me from a look which now and then came into her eyes that left but little doubt in my mind that she vaguely recalled the incident at the Pré Catelan with the cow.

It was a simple peasant dinner which followed.

When it was over, he went to a corner cupboard and drew forth a flat box of long perfectos, which I recognized instantly as the same brand of rare Havanas he had so extravagantly purchased from the Government. If I had had my doubt as to the identity of my man it was at rest now.

"You will find them mild," said he with a smile, as he lifted the tinfoil cover.

"No good cigar is strong," I replied, breaking the untouched row and bending my head as my host struck a match, my mind more on the scene in the Government's shop than the quality of his tobacco. And yet with all the charm that the atmosphere of his place afforded, two things still seemed to me strange — the absence of a servant, until I realized instinctively the incident of the balky cow, and the prompt bolting of the outside door.

The first I explained to myself as being due to her peasant blood and her ability to help herself; the second to the loneliness of the place and the characters it sometimes harboured. As for my host, I had to admit, despite my mental queries, that his bearing and manner completely captivated me, for a more delightful conversationalist it would have been difficult to find.

Not only did he know the art of eliminating himself and amusing you with topics that pleased you, but his cleverness in avoiding the personal was amazingly skilful. His tact was especially accentuated when, with a significant look at his companion, who at once rose from her seat and, crossing the room, busied herself with choosing the liqueurs from a closet in the corner of the room, he drew me aside by the fire, and in a calm, sotto voce said with intense earnestness:

"You may think it strange, monsieur, that I invited you, that I was even insistent. You, like myself, are a man of the world and can understand. You will do me a great favour if you will not mention to any one having met either myself or my little housekeeper" (there was not a tremor in his voice), "who, as you see, is a peasant; in fact, she was born here. We are not bothered with either friends or acquaintances here, nor do we care for prowlers; you

must excuse me for at first taking you for one.
You, of course, know the reputation of La
Poche."

"You could not have chosen a better place
to be lost in," I answered, smiling as discreetly
as one should over the confession of another's
love affair. "Moreover, in life I have found it
the best policy to keep one's mouth shut. You
have my word, monsieur — it is as if we had
never met — as if La Poche did not exist."

"Thank you," said he calmly, taking the tiny
liqueur glasses from her hands; "what will you
have — cognac or green chartreuse ?"

"Chartreuse," I answered quietly. My eye
had caught the labels which I knew to be genuine from the Grenoble printer.

"Ah! you knew it — *Dieu!* but it is good,
that old chartreuse!" exclaimed my hostess
with a rippling laugh as she filled my glass,
"we are lucky to find it."

Then something happened which even now
sends a cold chill down my spine. Hardly had
I raised my glass to my lips when there came a
sharp, determined rap at the bolted door, and

my host sprang to his feet. For a moment no
one spoke — I turned instinctively to look at
my lady of the Pré Catelan. She was breathing
with dilated eyes, her lips drawn and quivering,
every muscle of her lithe body trembling. He
was standing erect, his head thrown back, his
whole body tense. One hand gripped the
back of his chair, the other was outstretched
authoritatively toward us as if to command
our silence.

Again the rapping, this time violent, insistent.

"Who is there?" he demanded, after what
seemed to me an interminable moment of suspense.

With this he slipped swiftly through a door
leading into a narrow corridor, closed another
door at the end of the passage, broke the key in
the lock and returned on tiptoe as noiselessly as
he left the room. Then picking up the lamp he
placed it under the table, thus deadening its glow.

Now a voice rang out, "Open in the name
of the Law."

No one moved.

He again gripped the back of the chair, his

face deathly white, his jaw set, his eyes with a sullen gleam in them.

I turned to look at her. Her hands were outstretched on the table, her dilated eyes staring straight at the bolt as if her whole life depended on its strength.

Again came the command to open, this time in a voice that allowed no question as to the determination of the outsider:

"Open in the name of the Law."

No one moved or answered.

A crashing thud, from a heavy beam, snapped the bolt from its screws, another blow tore loose the door. Through the opening and over the débris sprang a short, broad-shouldered man in a gray suit, while three other heavily built men entered, barring the exit.

The woman screamed and fell forward on the table, her head buried in her clenched hands. The Baron faced the one in gray.

"What do you want?" he stammered in the voice of a ghost.

"You, Pedro Maceiö," said the man in the gray suit, in a low, even tone, "for the last trick you will pull off in some years; open up things, do you hear?   All of it, and quick."

The Brazilian did not reply; he stood behind his chair, eyeing sullenly the man in gray, who now held a revolver at a level with his heart.

Then the man in gray called to one of his men, his eye still on the banker. "Break in the door at the end of the passage."

With the quickness of a cat, the Brazilian grabbed the chair and with a swinging blow tried to fell his assailant and dash past him. The man in gray dodged and pocketed his weapon. The next instant he had his prisoner by the throat and had slammed him against the wall; then came the sharp click of a pair of handcuffs. The banker tripped and fell to the floor.

It had all happened so quickly that I was dazed as I looked on. What it was all about I did not know. It seemed impossible that my host, a man whose bank was well known in Paris, was really a criminal. Were the intruders from the police? Or was it a clever ruse of four determined burglars?

I began now to gather my wits and think of

myself, although so far not one of the intruders had taken the slightest notice of my presence.

One of the men was occupied in breaking open the door at the end of the corridor, while another stood guard over the now sobbing, hysterical woman. The fourth had remained at the open doorway.

As for the prisoner, who had now regained his feet, he had sunk into the chair he had used in defence and sat there staring at the floor, breathing in short gasps.

The man who had been ordered by his chief to break open the door at the end of the corridor, now returned and laid upon the dinner table two engraved metal plates, and a handful of new one-hundred-franc notes; some I noticed from where I sat were blank on one side. With the plates came the acrid stench of a broken bottle of acid.

"My God! Counterfeiting!" I exclaimed half aloud.

The Baron rose from his seat and stretched out his linked hands.

"She is innocent," he pleaded huskily, lifting

his eyes to the woman. I could not repress a feeling of profound pity for him.

The man in gray made no reply; instead he turned to me.

"I shall escort you, too, monsieur," he remarked coolly.

"Escort me? *Me?* What have I got to do with it, I'd like to know?" I cried, springing to my feet. "I wish to explain — to make clear to you — *clear*. I want you to understand that I stumbled here by the merest chance; that I never spoke to this man in my life until to-night, that I accepted his hospitality purely because I did not wish to offend him, although I had shot late and was in a hurry to get home."

He smiled quietly.

"Please do not worry," he returned, "we know all about you. You are the American. Your house is the old one by the marsh in Pont du Sable. I called on you this afternoon, but you were absent. I am really indebted to you if you do but know it. By following your tracks, monsieur, we stumbled on the nest we have so long been looking for. Permit me to hand you my card. My name is Guinard — Sous Chief of the Paris Police."

I breathed easier — things were clearing up.

"And may I ask, monsieur, how you knew I had gone in the direction of La Poche?" I inquired. That was still a mystery.

"You have a little maid," he replied; "and little maids can sometimes be made to talk."

He paused and then said slowly, weighing each word.

"Yes, that no doubt surprises you, but we follow every clue. You were both sportsmen; that, as you know, monsieur, is always a bond, and we had not long to wait, although it was too dark for us to be quite sure when you both passed me. It was the bolting of the door that clinched the matter for me. But for the absence of two of my men on another scent we should have disturbed you earlier. I must compliment you, monsieur, on your knowledge of chartreuse as well as your taste for good cigars; permit me to offer you another." Here he slipped his hand into his pocket and handed me a duplicate of the one I had been smoking.

"Twelve boxes, Maceiö, were there not? Not expensive, eh, when purchased with these?" and he spread out the identical bank-notes with which his prisoner had paid for them in the Government store on the boulevard.

"As for you, monsieur, it is only necessary that one of my men take your statement at your house; after that you are free.

"Come, Maceiö," and he shook the prisoner by the shoulder, "you take the midnight train with me back to Paris — you too, madame."

And so I say again, and this time you must agree with me, that strange happenings, often with a note of terror in them, occur now and then in my lost village by the sea.

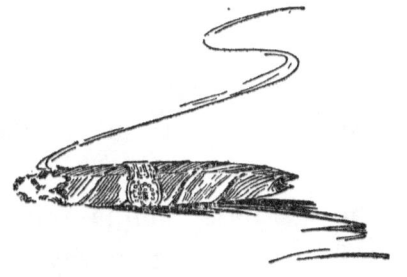

CHAPTER SEVEN

THE HORRORS OF WAR

A T THE very beginning of the straggling fish-ing-village of Pont du Sable and close by the tawny marsh stands the little stone house of the mayor. The house, like Monsieur le Maire himself, is short and sturdy. Its modest façade is half hidden under a coverlet of yellow roses that have spread at random over the tiled roof as high as the chimney. In front, edging the road, is a tidy strip of garden with more roses, a wood-pile, and an ancient well whose stone roof shelters a worn windlass that groans in protest whenever its chain and bucket are disturbed.

I heard the windlass complaining this sunny morning as I passed on my way through the village and caught sight of the ruddy mayor in his blue blouse lowering the bucket. The chain snapped taut, the bucket gulped its fill, and Monsieur le Maire caught sight of me.

"*Ah bigre!*" he exclaimed as he left the bucket where it hung and came forward with both hands outstretched in welcome, a smile wrinkling his genial face, clean-shaven to the edges of his short, cropped gray side-whiskers, reaching well beneath his chin. "Come in, come in," he insisted, laying a persuasive hand on my shoulder, as he unlatched his gate.

It is almost impossible for a friend to pass the mayor's without being stopped by just such a welcome. The twinkle in his eyes and the hearty genuineness of his greeting are irresistible. The next moment you have crossed his threshold and entered a square, low-ceiled room that for over forty years has served Monsieur le Maire as living room, kitchen, and executive chamber.

He had left me for a moment, as he always does when he welcomes a friend. I could hear from the pantry cupboard beyond the shivery tinkle of glasses as they settled on a tray. He had again insisted, as he always does, upon my occupying the armchair in the small parlour adjoining, with its wax flowers and its steel engraving of Napoleon at Waterloo; but I had protested as I always do, for I prefer the kitchen.

I like its cavernous fireplace with its crane and spit, and the low ceiling upheld by great beams of rough-hewn oak, and the tall clock in the corner, and the hanging copper saucepans, kettles and ladles, kept as bright as polished gold. Here, too, is a generous Norman armoire with carved oaken doors swung on barhinges of shining steel, and a centre-table provided with a small bottle of violet ink, a scratchy pen and an iron seal worked by a lever — a seal that has grown dull from long service in the stamping of certain documents relative to plain justice, marriage, the official recognition of the recently departed and the newly born. Above the fireplace hangs a faded photograph of a prize bull, for you must know that Monsieur le Maire has been for half a generation a dealer in Norman cattle.

Presently he returned with the tray, placing it upon the table within reach of our chairs while I stood admiring the bull.

He stopped as he half drew the cork from a fat brown jug, and looked at me curiously, his voice sinking almost to a whisper.

"You never were a dealer in beef?" he ventured timidly.

I shook my head sadly.

"*Hélas! Hélas!* Never mind," said he. "One cannot be everything. There's my brother-in-law, Péquin; he does not know a yearling from a three-year-old. It is he who keeps the little store at Saint Philippe."

The cork squeaked out. He filled the thimble glasses with rare old applejack so skilfully that another drop would have flushed over their worn gilt rims. What a gracious old gentleman he is! If it be a question of clipping a rose from his tidy garden and presenting it to a lady, he does it with such a gentle courtliness that the rose smells the sweeter for it — almost a lost art nowadays.

"I saw the curé this morning," he remarked,

as we settled ourselves for a chat. "He could not stop, but he waved me an *au revoir*, for he was in a hurry to catch his train. He had been all night in his duck-blind — I doubt if he had much luck, for the wind is from the south. There is a fellow for you who loves to shoot," chuckled the mayor.

"Some news for him of game?" I inquired.

The small eyes of the mayor twinkled knowingly. "*Entre nous*," he confided, "he has gone to Bonvilette to spray the sick roses of a friend with sulphate of iron — he borrowed my squirt-gun yesterday."

"And how far is it to Bonvilette?"

"*Eh ben!* One must go by the little train to Nivelle," explained Monsieur le Maire, "and from Nivelle to Bonvilette there lies a good twenty kilometres for a horse. Let us say he will be back in three days."

"And the mass meanwhile?" I ventured.

"*Mon Dieu!* What will you have? The roses of his old friend are sick. It is the duty of a curé to tend the sick. Besides ——"

Here Monsieur le Maire leaned forward within

reach of my ear, and I caught in whispers something relative to a château and one of the best
cellars of Bordeaux in France.

"Naturally," I replied, with a wink, and again
my eyes reverted to the prize bull.   It is not wise
to raise one's voice in so small a village as Pont
du Sable, even indoors.

"A pretty beast!" affirmed the mayor, noticing my continued interest in live stock.   "And
let me tell you that I took him to England in
'eighty-two. *Ah, mais oui! Hélas! Hélas!*
What a trip!" he sighed.   "Monsieur Toupinet
— he that has the big farm at Saint Philippe —
and I sailed together the third of October, in
1882, with forty steers.   Our ship was called
The Souvenir, and I want to tell you, my friend,
it wasn't gay, that voyage. *Ah, mais non!*
Toupinet was sea-sick — I was sea-sick — the
steers were sea-sick — all except that *sacré* brute
up there, and he roared all the way from Calais
to London. *Eh ben!*   And would you believe
it?"   At the approaching statement Monsieur
le Maire's countenance assumed a look of right-
eous indignation.   He raised his fist and brought

it down savagely on the table as he declared:
"Would you believe it? We were *thirty-four
hours* without eating and *twenty-nine hours,
mon Dieu!* without drinking!"

I looked up in pained astonishment.

"And that wasn't all," continued the mayor.
"A hurricane struck us three hours out, and we
rolled all night in a dog's sea. The steers were
up to their bellies in water. Aye, but she did
blow, and *The Souvenir* had all she could do to
keep afloat. The captain was lashed to the
bridge all night and most of the next day.
Neither Toupinet nor myself ever expected to
see land again, and there we were like calves in
a pen on the floor of the cabin full of tobacco-
smoke and English, and not a word of English
could we speak except 'yes' and 'good morning.'" Here Monsieur le Maire stopped and
choked. Finally he dried his eyes on the sleeve
of his blouse, for he was wheezing with laughter,
took a sip from his glass, and resumed:

"Well, the saints did not desert us. *Ah,
mais non!* For about four o'clock in the afternoon the captain sighted Su-Tum-Tum."

"Sighted what?" I exclaimed.

"*Eh ben!* Su-Tum-Tum," he replied.

"Where had you drifted? To the Corean coast?"

"*Mais non*," he retorted, annoyed at my dullness to comprehend. "We were saved — *comprenez-vous?* — for there, to starboard, lay Su-Tum-Tum as plain as a sheep's nose."

"England? Impossible!" I returned.

"*Mais parfaitement!*" he declared, with a hopeless gesture. "*Su-Tum-Tum*," he reiterated slowly for my benefit.

"Never heard of it," I replied.

The next instant he was out of his chair, and fumbling in a drawer of the table extracted a warped atlas, reseated himself, and began to turn the pages.

"*Eh, voilà!*" he cried as his forefinger stopped under a word along the English coast. "That's Su-Tum-Tum plain enough, isn't it?"

"Ah! Southampton!" I exclaimed. "Of course — plain as day."

"Ah!" ejaculated the mayor, leaning back in his chair with a broad smile of satisfaction.

"You see, I was right, Su-Tum-Tum. *Eh ben!* Do you know," he said gently as I left him, "when you first came to Pont du Sable there were times then, my poor friend, when I could not understand a word you said in French."

Then, as if a sudden thought had struck him, he called me back as he closed the gate.

"Are those gipsies still camped outside your wall?" he inquired, suddenly assuming the dignity of his office. "*Bon Dieu!* They are a bad lot, those vagabonds! If I don't tell them to be off you won't have a duck or a chicken left."

"Let them stay," I pleaded, "they do no harm. Besides, I like to see the light of their camp-fire at night scurrying over my wall."

"How many are there?" inquired his excellency.

"Seven or eight, not counting the dogs chained under the wagons," I confessed reluctantly, fearing the hand of the law, for I have a fondness for gipsies. "But you need not worry about them. They won't steal from me. Their wagons are clean inside and out."

"*Ah, mais!*" sighed the mayor. "It's just

like you. You spoil your cat, you spoil your dog, and now you're spoiling these rascals by giving them a snug berth. Have they their papers of identity?"

"Yes," I called back, "the chief showed them to me when he asked permission to camp."

"Of course," laughed the mayor. "You'll never catch them without them — signed by officials we never can trace."

He waved me a cheery *au revoir* and returned to the well of the groaning windlass while I continued on my way through the village.

Outside the squat stone houses, nets were drying in the sun. Save for the occasional rattle of a passing cart, the village was silent, for these fisher-folk go barefooted. Presently I reached the public square, where nothing ever happens, and, turning an iron handle, entered Pont du Sable's only store. A box of a place, smelling of dried herring, kerosene, and cheese; and stocked with the plain necessities — almost everything, from lard, tea, and big nails to soap, tarpaulins, and applejack. The night's catch of mackerel had been good, and the small room

with its zinc bar was noisy with fisher-folk —
wiry fishermen with legs and chests as hard as
iron; slim brown fisher girls as hardy as the men,
capricious, independent and saucy; a race of
blonds for the most part, with the temperament
of brunettes. Old women grown gray and
leathery from fighting the sea, and old men too
feeble to go — one of these hung himself last
winter because of this.

It was here, too, I found Marianne, dripping
wet, in her tarpaulins.

"What luck?" I asked her as I helped myself
to a package of cigarettes from a pigeonhole and
laid the payment thereof on the counter.

"*Eh ben!*" she laughed. "We can't complain. If the good God would send us such
fishing every night we should eat well enough."

She strode through the group to the counter
to thrust out an empty bottle.

"Eight sous of the best," she demanded
briskly of the mild-eyed grocer. "My man's
as wet as a rat — he needs some fire in him and
he'll feel as fit as a marquis."

A good catch is a tonic to Pont du Sable.

Instantly a spirit of good humour and camaraderie spreads through the village — even old scores are forgotten. A good haul of mackerel means a let-up in the daily struggle for existence, which in winter becomes terrible. The sea knows not charity. It massacres when it can and adds you to the line of dead things along its edge where you are only remembered by the ebb and flow of the tide. On blue calm mornings, being part of the jetsam, you may glisten in the sun beside a water-logged spar; at night you become a nonentity, of no more consequence along the wavering line of drift than a rotten gull. But if, like Marianne, you have fought skilfully, you may again enter Pont du Sable with a quicker eye, a harder body, and a deeper knowledge of the southwest gale.

Within the last week Pont du Sable has undergone a transformation. The dead village is alive with soldiers, for it is the time of the manœuvres. Houses, barns and cow-sheds are filled by night with the red-trousered infantry of the French *République*. By day, the window panes shiver under the distant flash and roar of artillery. The air vibrates with the rip and rattle of musketry — savage volleys, filling the heavens with shrill, vicious waves of whistling bullets that kill at a miraculous distance. It is well that all this murderous fire occurs beyond the desert of dunes skirting the open sea, for they say the result upon the iron targets on the marsh is something frightful. The general in command is in a good humour over the record.

Despatch-bearers gallop at all hours of the day and night through Pont du Sable's single street. The band plays daily in the public square. Sunburned soldiers lug sacks of provisions and bundles of straw out to five hundred more men bivouacked on the dunes. Whole regiments return to the little fishing-village at twilight singing gay songs, followed by the fisher girls.

> Ah! Mesdames—voilà du bon fromage!
> Celui qui l'a fait il est de son village!
> Voilà du bon fromage au lait!
> Il est du pays de celui qui l'a fait.

Three young officers are stopping at Monsieur le Curé's, who has returned from the sick

roses of his friend; and Tanrade has a colonel
and two lieutenants beneath his roof. As for
myself and the house abandoned by the marsh,
we are very much occupied with a blustering old
general, his aide-de-camp, and two common
soldiers; but I tremble lest the general should
discover the latter two, for you see, they knocked
at my door for a lodging before the general
arrived, and I could not refuse them. Both of
them put together would hardly make a full-
sized warrior, and both play the slide-trombone
in the band. Naturally their artistic temperament revolted at the idea of sleeping in the only
available place left in the village — a cow-shed
with cows. They explained this to me with so
many polite gestures, mingled with an occasional
salute at their assured gratefulness should I
acquiesce, that I turned them over for safe keeping to Suzette, who has given them her room
and sleeps in the garret. Suzette is overjoyed.
Dream of dreams! For Suzette to have one
real live soldier in the house — but to have two!
Both of these red-eared, red-trousered dispen-
sers of harmony are perfect in deportment, and

as quiet as mice. They slip out of my back gate at daylight, bound for the seat of war and slip in again at sundown like obedient children, talk in kitchen whispers to Suzette over hot cakes and cider, and go punctually to bed at nine — the very hour when the roaring old general and his aide-de-camp are toasting their gold spurs before my fire.

The general is tall and broad-shouldered, and as agile as a boy. There is a certain hard, compact firmness about him as if he had been cast in bronze. His alert eyes are either flashing in authority or beaming in gentleness. The same play between dominant roughness and tenderness is true, too, of his voice and manner.

"Madame," he said, last night, after dinner, as he bent and graciously kissed Alice de Bréville's hand, "forgive an old savage who pays you homage and the assurance of his profound respect." The next moment my courtyard without rocked with his reprimand to a bungling lieutenant.

To-night the general is an in uproar of good
humour after a storm, for did not some vagabonds steal the danger-posts intended to warn
the public of the location of the firing-line, so
that new ones had to be sent for? When the
news of the theft reached him his rage was something to behold. I could almost hear the little
slide-trombonists shake as far back as Suzette's
kitchen. Fortunately, the cyclone was of short
duration — to-night he is pleased over the good
work of his men during the days of mock war-
fare and at the riddled, twisted targets, all of
which is child's play to this veteran who has
weathered so many real battles.

To-night he has dined well, and his big hand
is stroking the Essence of Selfishness who purrs
against his medalled chest under a caress as gentle
as a woman's. He sings his favourite airs from
"Faust" and "Aïda" with gusto, and roars over
the gallant stories of his aide-de-camp, who,
being from the south of *La belle France*, is
never at a loss for a tale — tales that make the
general's medals twinkle merrily in the firelight.
It is my first joyful experience as host to the

military, but I cannot help being nervous over Suzette and the trombonists.

"Bah! Those *sacré* musicians!" exclaimed the general to-night as he puffed at his cigarette. "If there's a laggard in my camp, you may be sure it is one of those little devils with a horn or a whistle. *Mon Dieu!* Once during the manœuvres outside of Périgord I found three of them who refused to sleep on the ground — stole off and begged a lodging in a château, *parbleu!*"

"Ah — indeed ?" I stammered meekly.

"Yes, they did," he bellowed, "but I cured them." I saw the muscles in his neck flush crimson, and tried to change the subject, but in vain.

"If they do that in time of peace, they'll do the same in war," he thundered.

"Naturally," I murmured, my heart in my throat. The aide-de-camp grunted his approval while the general ran his hand over the gray bristles on his scarred head.

"Favours!" roared the general. "Favours, eh ? When my men sleep on the ground in rough weather, I sleep with them. What sort of discipline do you suppose I'd have if I did not share their hardships time and time again? Winter campaigns, forced marches — twenty-four hours of it sometimes in mountain snow. Bah! That is nothing! They need that training to go through worse, and yet those good fellows of mine, heavily loaded, never complain. I've seen it so hot, too, that it would melt a man's boots. It is always one of those imbeciles, then, with nothing heavier to carry than a clarinet, who slips off to a comfortable farm."

"*Bien entendu, mon général!*" agreed his aide-de-camp tersely as he leaned forward and kindled a fresh cigarette over the candle-shade.

Happily I noticed at that moment that the cigarette-box needed replenishing. It was an excuse at least to leave the room. A moment later I had tiptoed to the closed kitchen door and stood listening. Suzette was laughing. The trombonists were evidently very much at ease. They, too, were laughing. Little pleasantries

filtered through the crack in the heavy door that
made me hold my breath. Then I heard the
gurgle of cider poured into a glass, followed
swiftly by what I took to be unmistakably a
kiss.

It was all as plain now as Su-Tum-Tum. I
dared not break in upon them. Had I opened
the door, the general might have recognized their
voices. Meanwhile, silly nothings were demoral-
izing the heart of my good Suzette. She would
fall desperately in love with either one or the
other of those *sacré* virtuosos. Then another
thought struck me! One of them might be
Suzette's sweetheart, hailing from her own village, the manœuvres at Pont du Sable a lucky
meeting for them. A few sentences that I now
hurriedly caught convinced me of my own dense-
ness in not having my suspicions aroused when
they singled out my domain and begged my
hospitality.

The situation was becoming critical. By the
light of the crack I scribbled the following:

"Get those two imbeciles of yours hidden in
the hay-loft, quick. The general wants to see

the kitchen," and slipped it under the door, coughing gently in warning.

There was an abrupt silence — the sound of Suzette's slippered feet — and the scrap of paper disappeared. Then heavy, excited breathing within.

I dashed upstairs and was down again with the cigarettes before the general had remarked my tardiness to his aide. At midnight I lighted their candles and saw them safely up to bed. Then I went to my room fronting the marsh and breathed easier.

"Her sweetheart from her own village," I said to myself as I blew out my candle. "The other" — I sighed drowsily — "was evidently his cousin. The mayor was right. I have a bad habit of spoiling people and pets."

Then again my mind reverted to the general. What if he discovered them? My only consolation now was that to-day had seen the end of the manœuvres, and the soldiers would depart by a daylight train in the morning. I recalled, too, the awkward little speech of thanks for my hospitality the trombonists had made to me at an opportune moment before dinner. Finally I fell into a troubled sleep.

Suzette brought me my coffee at seven.

"Luckily the general did not discover them!" I exclaimed when Suzette had closed the double door of my bedroom.

"*Mon Dieu!* What danger we have run!" whispered the little maid. "I could not sleep, monsieur, thinking of it."

"You got them safely to the haymow?" I inquired anxiously.

"Oh! *Mais oui*, monsieur. But then they slept over the cider-press back of the big casks. Monsieur advised the hay-loft, but they said the roof leaked. And had it rained, monsieur ——"

"See here," I interrupted, eyeing her trim self from head to foot savagely. "You've known that little devil with the red ears before."

I saw Suzette pale.

"Confess!" I exclaimed hoarsely, with a military gesture of impatience. "He comes from your village. Is it not so, my child?"

Suzette was silent, her plump hands twisting nervously at her apron pocket.

"I am right, am I not? I might have guessed as much when they came."

"Oh, monsieur!" Suzette faltered, the tears welling up from the depths of her clear trustful eyes.

"Is it not so?" I insisted.

"Oh! Oh! *Mon Dieu, oui*," she confessed half audibly. "He — he is the son of our neighbor, Monsieur Jacot."

"At Saint Philippe?"

"At Saint Philippe, monsieur. We were children together, Gaston and I. I — I — was glad to see him again, monsieur," sobbed the little maid. "He is very nice, Gaston."

"When are you to be married?" I ventured after a moment's pause.

"*Ben — eh ben!* In two years, monsieur — after Gaston finishes his military service. He —he — has a good trade, monsieur."

"Soloist?" I asked grimly.

"No, monsieur — tailor for ladies. We shall live in Paris," she added, and for an instant

her eyes sparkled; then again their gaze reverted
to the now sadly twisted apron pocket, for I
was silent.

"No more Suzette then!" I said to myself.
No more merry, willing little maid-of-all-work!
No more hot mussels steaming in a savory sauce!
Her purée of peas, her tomato farcies, the stuffed
artichokes, and her coffee the like of which never
before existed, would vanish with the rest. But
true love cannot be argued. There was nothing
to do but to hold out my hand in forgiveness. As
I did so the general rang for his coffee.

"*Mon Dieu!*" gasped Suzette. "He rings."
And flew down to her kitchen.

An hour later the general was sauntering leisurely up the road through the village over his
morning cigar. The daylight train, followed
rapidly by four extra sections, had cleared Pont
du Sable of all but two of the red-trousered
infantry — my trombonists! They had arrived
an hour and twenty minutes late, winded and
demoralized. They sat together outside the
locked station unable to speak, pale and panic-
stricken.

The first object that caught the general's eye as he slowly turned into the square by the little station was their four red-trousered legs — then he caught the glint of their two brass trombones The next instant heads appeared at the windows. It was as if a bomb had suddenly exploded in the square.

The two trombonists were now on their feet, shaking from head to foot while they saluted their general, whose ever-approaching stride struck fresh agony to their hearts.   He was roaring:

"*Canailles! Imbéciles!*   A month of prison!" and "*Sacré bon Dieu's!*" were all jumbled together.   "Overslept!   Overslept, did you?" he bellowed.   "In a château, I'll wager.   *Parbleu!*   Where then?   Out with it!"

"*Pardon, mon général!*" chattered Gaston. "It was in the stone house of the American gentleman by the marsh."

We lunched together in my garden at noon. He had grown calm again under the spell of the Burgundy, but Suzette, I feared, would be ill.

"Come, be merciful," I pleaded.

"He is the fiancé of my good Suzette; besides, you must not forget that you were all my guests."

The general shrugged his shoulders helplessly. "They were lucky to have gotten off with a month!" he snapped. "You saw that those little devils were handcuffed?" he asked of his aide.

"Yes, my general, the gendarme attended to them."

"You were my guests," I insisted. "Hold me responsible if you wish."

"Hold *you* responsible!" he exclaimed. "But you are a foreigner — it would be a little awkward."

"It is my good Suzette," I continued, "that I am thinking of."

He leaned back in his chair, and for a moment again ran his hands thoughtfully over the bristles of his scarred head. He had a daughter of his own.

"The coffee," I said gently to my unhappy Suzette as she passed.

"*Oui! Oui*, monsieur," she sighed, then suddenly mustering up her courage, she gasped:

"*Oh, mon général!* Is it true, then, that Gaston must go to jail? *Ah! Mon Dieu!*"

"*Eh bien*, my girl! It will not kill him, *Sapristi!* He will be a better soldier for it."

"Be merciful," I pleaded.

"*Eh bien! Eh bien!*" he retorted. "*Eh bien!*" And cleared his throat.

"Forgive them," I insisted. "They overslept. I don't want Suzette to marry a jail-bird."

Again he scratched his head and frowned. Suzette was in tears.

"Um! Difficult!" he grumbled. "Order for arrest once given ——" Then he shot a glance at me. I caught a twinkle in his eye.

"*Eh bien!*" he roared. "There — I forgive them! Ah, those *sacré* musicians!"

Suzette stood there trembling, unable even to thank him, the colour coming and going in her peasant cheeks.

"Are they free, general?" I asked.

"Yes," he retorted, "both of them."

"Bravo!" I exclaimed.

"Understand that I have done it for the little girl — and *you*. Is that plain?"

"Perfectly," I replied. "As plain as Su-Tum-Tum!" I added under my breath as I filled his empty glass in gratefulness to the brim.

"Halt!" shouted the general as the happiest of Suzettes turned toward her kitchen.

"Eh — um!" he mumbled awkwardly in a voice that had suddenly grown thick. Then he sprang to his feet and raised his glass.

"A health to the bride!" he cried.

CHAPTER EIGHT

THE MILLION OF MONSIEUR DE SAVIGNAC

THE bay of Pont du Sable, which the incoming tide had so swiftly filled at daylight, now lay a naked waste of oozing black mud. The birds had gone with the receding sea, and I was back from shooting, loafing over my pipe and coffee in a still corner among the roses of my wild garden, hidden behind the old wall, when that Customhouse soldier-gardener of mine, Pierre, appeared with the following message:

"Monsieur de Savignac presents his salutations the most distinguished and begs that monsieur will give him the pleasure of calling on him *à propos* of the little spaniel."

What an unexpected and welcome surprise! For weeks I had hunted in vain for a thorough-

bred.   I had never hoped to be given one from
the kennels of Monsieur de Savignac's château.

"Enchanted,   Pierre!"   I   cried — "Present
my   compliments   to   Monsieur   de   Savignac.
Tell him how sincerely grateful I am, and say
that he may expect me to-morrow before noon."

I   could   easily   imagine   what   a   beauty   my
spaniel would be, clean-limbed and alert like
the   ones   in   the   coloured   lithographs.   "No
wonder," I thought, as Pierre left me, "that
every   peasant   for   miles   around   spoke   of   this
good   Monsieur   de   Savignac's   generosity.   Here
he was giving me a dog.   To me, his American
neighbour, whom he had never met!"

As I walked over to the château with Pierre
the   next   morning,   I   recalled   to   my   mind   the
career   of   this   extraordinary   man,   whose   only
vice was his great generosity.

When Monsieur de Savignac was twenty-one
he inherited a million francs, acquired a high hat
with a straight brim, a standing collar, well open
at   the   throat   (in   fashion   then   under   Napoleon
III.), a flowing cravat — a plush waistcoat with
crystal   buttons,   a   plum-coloured   broadcloth

coat and trousers of a pale lemon shade, striped
with black, gathered tight at the ankles, their
bottoms flouncing over a pair of patent-leather
boots with high heels.

He was tall, strong and good-natured, this
lucky Jacques de Savignac, with a weakness
for the fair sex which was appalling, and a charm
of manner as irresistible as his generosity. A
clumsy fencer, but a good comrade — a fellow
who could turn a pretty compliment, danced
better than most of the young dandies at court,
drove his satin-skinned pair of bays through the
Bois with an easy smile, and hunted hares when
the shooting opened with the dogged tenacity
of a veteran poacher.

When he was twenty-one, the Paris that
Grévin drew was in the splendour of an extravagant life that she was never to see again, and
never has. One could *amuse* one's self then —
ah! *Dame, oui!*

There is no emperor now to keep Paris gay.

What suppers at Véfour's! What a brilliant life
there was in those days under the arcades of the
dear old Palais Royal, the gay world going daily

to this mondaine cloister to see and be seen —
to dine and wine — to make conquests of the
heart and dance daylight quadrilles.

Paris was ordered to be daily *en fête* and the
host at the Tuileries saw to it that the gaiety
did not flag. It was one way at least from keeping the populace from cutting one another's
throats, which they did later with amazing
ferocity.

There were in those good old days under
Louis Napoleon plenty of places to gamble and
spend the inherited gold. Ah! it was Rabe-
laisian enough! What an age to have been
the recipient of a million at twenty-one! It was
like being a king with no responsibilities. No
wonder de Savignac left the university — he
had no longer any need of it. He dined now
at the Maison Dorée and was seen nightly at
the "Bal Mabille" or the "Closerie des Lilas,"
focussing his gold-rimmed monocle on the flying
feet and lace *frou-frou* of "Diane la Sournoise,"
or roaring with laughter as he chucked gold
louis into the satined lap of some "Francine"
or "Cora" amid the blare of the band, and the

flash of jewels strung upon fair arms and fairer necks of woman who went nightly to the "Bal Mabille" in smart turnouts and the costliest gowns money could buy — and after the last mad quadrille was ended, on he went to supper at Bignon's where more gaiety reigned until blue dawn, and where the women were still laughing and merry and danced as easily on the table as on the floor.

What a time, I say, to have inherited a million! And how many good friends he had! Painters and musicians, actors and wits (and there *were* some in those days) — no king ever gathered around him a jollier band.

It was from one of these henchmen of his that de Savignac purchased his château (long since emptied of its furniture) — from a young nobleman pressed hard for his debts, like most young noblemen are — and so the great château close to my Village of Vagabonds, and known for miles around, became de Savignac's.

What house parties he gave then! — men and women of talent flocked under his hospitable roof — indeed there was no lack of talent —

some of it from the Opéra — some of it from
the Conservatoire, and they brought their voices
and their fiddles with them and played and sang
for him for days, in exchange for his feudal
hospitality — more than that, the painter Paul
Deschamps covered the ceiling of his music
room with chubby cupids playing golden
trumpets and violins — one adorable little fellow in the cove above the grand piano struggling
with a 'cello twice as high as himself, and Carin
painted the history of love in eight panels upon
the walls of the old ballroom, whose frescoes
were shabby enough, so I am told, when de
Savignac purchased them.

There were times also when the château
was full to overflowing with guests, so that the
late comers were often quartered in a low two-
story manor close by, that nestled under great
trees — a cosey, dear old place covered with ivy
and climbing yellow roses, with narrow alleys
leading to it flanked by tall poplars, and a formal
garden behind it in the niches of whose surrounding wall were statues of Psyche and Venus,
their smooth marble shoulders stained by rain

and the drip and ooze of growing things. One of them even now, still lifts its encrusted head to the weather.

During the shooting season there were weeks when he and his guests shot daily from the crack of dawn until dark, the game-keepers following with their carts that by night were loaded with hares, partridges, woodcock and quail — then such a good dinner, sparkling with repartee and good wine, and laughter and dancing after it, until the young hours in the morning. One was more solid in those days than now — tired as their dogs after the day's hunt, they dined and danced themselves young again for the morrow.

And what do you think they did after the Commune? They made him mayor. Yes, indeed, to honour him — Mayor of Hirondelette, the little village close to his estate, and de Savignac had to be formal and dignified for the first time in his life — this good Bohemian — at the village fêtes, at the important meetings of the Municipal Council, composed of a dealer in cattle, the blacksmith and the notary. Again, in time of marriage, accident or death, and annually at the school exercises, when he presented prizes to the children spic and span for the occasion, with voices awed to whispers, and new shoes. And he loved them all — all those dirty little brats that had been scrubbed clean, and their ruddy cheeks polished like red apples, to meet "Monsieur le Maire."

He was nearing middle life now, but he was not conscious of it, being still a bachelor. There was not as yet, a streak of gray in his well-kept beard, and the good humour sparkled in his merry eyes as of old. The only change that had occurred concerned the million. It was no longer the brilliant solid million of his youth. It was sadly torn off in places — there were also several large holes in it — indeed, if the truth be told, it was little more than a remnant of its once splendid entirety. It had been eaten by moths — certain shrewd old wasps, too, had nested in it for years — not a sou of it had vanished in speculation or bad investment. Monsieur de Savignac (this part of it the curé told me) was as ignorant as a child concerning

business affairs and stubbornly avoided them.
He had placed his fortune intact in the Bank of
France, and had drawn out what he needed for
his friends.   In the first year of his inheritance
he glanced at the balance statement sent him by
the bank, with a feeling of peaceful delight.   As
the years of his generosity rolled on, he avoided
reading it at all — "like most optimists,"
remarked the curé, "he did not wish to know
the truth."   At forty-six he married the niece
of an impoverished old wasp, a gentleman still
in excellent health, owing to de Savignac's
generosity.   It was his good wife now, who
read the balance statement.

For a while after his marriage, gaiety again
reigned at the château, but upon a more
economical basis; then gradually they grew
to entertain less and less; indeed there were
few left of the moths and old wasps to give
to — they had flown to cluster around another
million.

Most of this Pierre, who was leading me
through the leafy lane that led to de Savignac's
home, knew or could have known, for it was

common talk in the country around, but his
mind to-day was not on de Savignac's past,
but on the dog which we both were so anxious
to see.

"Monsieur has never met Monsieur de Savignac?" ventured Pierre as we turned our steps
out of the brilliant sunlight, and into a wooded
path skirting the extensive forest of the estate.

"Not yet, Pierre."

"He is a fine old gentleman," declared Pierre,
discreetly lowering his voice. "Poor man!"

"Why *poor*, Pierre?" I laughed, "with an
estate like this — nonsense!"

"Ah! Monsieur does not know?" — Pierre's
voice sunk to a whisper — "the château is
mortgaged, monsieur. There is not a tree or
a field left Monsieur de Savignac can call his
own. Do you know, monsieur, he has no
longer even the right to shoot over the ground?
Monsieur sees that low roof beyond with the
single chimney smoking — just to the left of the
château towers?"

I nodded.

"That is where Monsieur de Savignac **now**
lives.   It is called the garçonnière."

"But the château, Pierre?"

"It is rented to a Peruvian gentleman, **mon-**
sieur, who takes in boarders."

"Pierre!" I exclaimed, "we go no farther.   **I**
knew nothing of this.   I am not going to accept
a dog from a gentleman in Monsieur de Savignac's unfortunate circumstances.   It is not
right.   No, no.   Go and present my deep
regrets to Monsieur de Savignac and tell him —
tell him what you please.   Say that my rich
uncle has just sent me a pair of pointers —
that I sincerely appreciate his generous offer,
that ——"

Pierre's small black eyes opened as wide as
possible.   He shrugged his shoulders twice and
began twisting thoughtfully the waxed ends of
his moustache to a finer point.

"Pardon, monsieur," he resumed after an
awkward pause, "but — but monsieur, by not
going, will grieve Monsieur de Savignac —   He
will be so happy to give monsieur the dog — so
happy, monsieur.   If Monsieur de Savignac

could not give something to somebody he would die. Ah, he gives everything away, that good Monsieur de Savignac!" exclaimed Pierre. "I was once groom in his stables — *oui*, monsieur, and he married us when he was Mayor of Hirondelette, and he paid our rent — *oui*, monsieur, and the doctor and . . . "

"We'll proceed, Pierre," said I. "A man of de Savignac's kind in the world is so rare that one should do nothing to thwart him."

We walked on for some distance along the edge of a swamp carpeted with strong ferns. Presently we came to a cool, narrow alley flanked and roofed by giant poplars. At the end of this alley a wicket gate barred the entrance to the courtyard of the garçonnière.

As we drew nearer I saw that its ancient two-story façade was completely covered by the climbing mass of ivy and yellow roses, the only openings being the Louis XIV. windows, and the front door, flush with the gravelled court, bordered by a thick hedge of box.

"Monsieur the American gentleman for the dog," announced Pierre to the boy servant in a

blue apron who appeared to open the wicket
gate.

A moment later the door of the garçonnière
opened, and a tall, heavily built man with silver
white hair and beard came forth to greet me.

I noticed that the exertion of greeting me
made him short of breath, and that he held his
free hand for a second pressed against his heart
as he ushered me across his threshold and into
a cool, old-fashioned sitting room, the walls
covered with steel engravings, the furniture
upholstered in green rep.

"Have the goodness to be seated, monsieur,"
he insisted, waving me to an armchair, while he
regained his own, back of an old-fashioned
desk.

"Ah! The — little — dog," he began, slowly
regaining his breath. "You are all the time
shooting, and I heard you wanted one. It is
so difficult to get a really — good — dog —
in this country. "François!" he exclaimed,
"You may bring in the little dog — and, François!" he added, as the boy servant turned ,to
go — "bring glasses and a bottle of Musigny

— you will find it on the shelf back of the
Medoc." Then he turned to me: "There are
still two bottles left," and he laughed heartily.

"Bien, monsieur," answered the boy, and
departed with a key big enough to have opened
a jail.

The moment had arrived for me to draw
forth a louis, which I laid on his desk in accord-
ance with an old Norman custom, still in vogue
when you accept as a gift a dog from an estate.

"Let your domestics have good cheer and
wine to-night," said I.

"Thank you," he returned with sudden
formality. "I shall put it aside for them," and
he dropped the gold piece into a small drawer
of his desk.

I did not know until Pierre, who was waiting
outside in the court, told me afterwards, that his
entire staff of servants was composed of the boy
with the blue apron and the cook — an old
woman — the last of his faithful servitors, who
now appeared with a tray of trembling glasses,
followed by the boy, the dusty cobwebbed bottle
of rare Musigny and — my dog!

Not a whole dog. But a flub-dub little spaniel puppy — very blond — with ridiculously long ears, a double-barrelled nose, a roly-poly stomach and four heavy unsteady legs that got in his way as he tried to navigate in a straight line to make my acquaintance.

"*Voilà!*" cried de Savignac. "Here he is. He'll make an indefatigable hunter, like his mother — wait until he is two years old — He'll stand to his day's work beside the best in France ——"

"And what race is he? may I ask, Monsieur de Savignac."

"Gorgon — Gorgon of Poitou," he returned with enthusiasm. "They are getting as rare now as this," he declared, nodding to the cobwebbed bottle, as he rose, drew the cork, and filled my glass.

While we sipped and chatted, his talk grew merry with chuckles and laughter, for he spoke of the friends of his youth, who played for him and sang to him — the thing which he loved most of all, he told me. "Once," he confessed to me, "I slipped away and travelled to

Hungary. Ah! how those good gipsies played
for me there! I was drunk with their music for
two weeks. It is stronger than wine, that music
of the gipsies," he said knowingly.

Again our talk drifted to hunting, of the good
old times when hares and partridges were plenti-
ful, and so he ran on, warmed by the rare
Musigny, reminiscing upon the old days and
his old friends who were serious sportsmen, he
declared, and knew the habits of the game they
were after, for they seldom returned with an
empty game-bag.

"And you are just as keen about shooting as
ever?" I ventured.

"I shoot no more," he exclaimed with a
shrug. "One must be a philosopher when one
is past sixty — when one has no longer the solid
legs to tramp with, nor the youth and the diges-
tion to *live*. Ah! Besides, the life has changed
— Paris was gay enough in my day. I *lived*
then, but at sixty — I stopped — with my memories. No! no! beyond sixty it is quite impossible. One must be philosophic, eh?"

Before I could reply, Madame de Savignac

entered the room. I felt the charm of her personality, as I looked into her eyes, and as she welcomed me I forgot that her faded silk gown was once in fashion before I was born, or that madame was short and no longer graceful. As the talk went on, I began to study her more at my ease, when some one rapped at the outer door of the vestibule. She started nervously, then, rising, whispered to François, who had come to open it, then a moment later rose again and, going out into the hall, closed the door behind her.

"Thursday then," I heard a man's gruff voice reply brusquely.

I saw de Savignac straighten in his chair, and lean to one side as if trying to catch a word of the muffled conversation in the vestibule. The next instant he had recovered his genial manner to me, but I saw that again he laboured for some moments painfully for his breath.

The door of the vestibule closed with a vicious snap. Then I heard the crunch of sabots on the gravelled court, and the next instant caught a glimpse of the stout, brutal figure of the peasant Le Gros, the big dealer in cattle, as he passed the narrow window of the vestibule.

It was *he*, then, with his insolent, bestial face purple with good living, who had slammed the door. I half started indignantly from my chair — then I remembered it was no affair of mine.

Presently madame returned — flushed, and, with a forced smile, in which there was more pain than pleasure, poured for me another glass of Musigny. I saw instantly that something unpleasant had passed — something unusually unpleasant — perhaps tragic, and I discreetly rose to take my leave.

Without a word of explanation as to what had happened, Madame de Savignac kissed my dog good-bye on the top of his silky head, while de Savignac stroked him tenderly. He was perfectly willing to come with me, and cocked his head on one side.

We were all in the courtyard now.

"*Au revoir*," they waved to me.

"*Au revoir*," I called back.

"*Au revoir*," came back to me faintly, as Pierre and the doggie and I entered the green lane and started for home.

"Monsieur sees that I was right, is it not true?" ventured Pierre, as we gained the open fields. "Monsieur de Savignac would have been grieved had not monsieur accepted the little dog."

"Yes," I replied absently, feeling more like a marauder for having accepted all they had out of their hearts thrust upon me.

Then I stopped — lifted the roly-poly little spaniel, and taking him in my arms whispered under his silky ear: "We shall go back often, you and I"— and I think he understood.

A few days later I dropped into Madame Vinet's snug little café in Pont du Sable. It was early in the morning and the small room of the café, with barely space enough for its four tables still smelt of fresh soap suds and hot water. At one of the tables sat the peasant in his black blouse, sipping his coffee and apple-jack.

Le Gros lifted his sullen face as I entered, shifted his elbows, gripped the clean marble slab of his table with both his red hands, and with a shrewd glint from his small, cruel eyes, looked up and grunted.

"Ah! — *bonjour*, monsieur."

"*Bonjour*, Monsieur Le Gros," I replied. "We seem to be the only ones here. Where's the patronne?"

"Upstairs, making her bed — another dry day," he muttered, half to himself, half to me.

"She will stay dry for some days," I returned. "The wind is well set from the northeast."

"*Sacristi!* a dirty time," he growled. "My steers are as dry as an empty cask."

"I'd like a little rain myself," said I, reaching for a chair — "I have a young dog to train — a spaniel Monsieur de Savignac has been good enough to give me. He is too young to learn to follow a scent on dry ground."

Le Gros raised his bull-like head with a jerk.

"De Savignac gave you a *dog*, did he? and he has a dog to give away, has he?"

The words came out of his coarse throat with a snarl.

I dropped the chair and faced him.

(He is the only man in Pont du Sable that I positively dislike.)

"Yes," I declared, "he gave me a dog. May I ask you what business it is of yours?"

A flash of sullen rage illumined for a moment the face of the cattle dealer. Then he muttered something in his peasant accent and sat glowering into his empty coffee cup as I turned and left the room, my mind reverting to Madame de Savignac's door which his coarse hand had closed with a vicious snap.

We took the short cut across the fields often now — my yellow puppy and I. Indeed I grew to see these good friends of mine almost daily, and as frequently as I could persuade them, they came to my house abandoned by the marsh.

The Peruvian gentleman's boarding house had been a failure, and I learned from the curé that the de Savignacs were hard pressed to pay their creditors.

It was Le Gros who held the mortgage, I further gleaned.

And yet those two dear people kept a brave heart. They were still giving what they had, and she kept him in ignorance as best she could, softening the helplessness of it all, with her gentleness and her courage.

In his vague realization that the end was near, there were days when he forced himself into a gay mood and would come chuckling down the lane to open the gate for me, followed by Mirza, the tawny old mother of my puppy, who kept her faithful brown eyes on his every movement. Often it was she who sprang nimbly ahead and unlatched the gate for me with her paw and muzzle, an old trick he had taught her, and he would laugh when she did it, and tell me there were no dogs nowadays like her.

Thus now and then he forced himself to forget the swarm of little miseries closing down upon him — forgot even his aches and pains, due largely to the dampness of the vine-smothered garçonnière whose old-fashioned interior smelt of cellar damp, for there was hardly a room in it whose wall paper had escaped the mould.

It was not until March that the long-gathering storm broke — as quick as a crackling lizard of lightning strikes. Le Gros had foreclosed the mortgage.

The Château of Hirondelette was up for sale.

When de Savignac came out to open the gate for me late that evening his face was as white as the palings in the moonlight.

"Come in," said he, forcing a faint laugh — he stopped for a moment as he closed and locked the gate — labouring painfully for his breath. Then he slipped his arm under my own. "Come along," he whispered, struggling for his voice. "I have found another bottle of Musigny."

A funeral, like a wedding or an accident, is quickly over. The sale of de Savignac's château consumed three days of agony.

As I passed the "garçonnière" by the lane beyond the courtyard on my way to the last day's sale, I looked over the hedge and saw that the shutters were closed — farther on, a doctor's

gig was standing by the gate.   From a bent old
peasant woman in sabots and a white cap, who
passed, I learned which of the two was ill.   It
was as I had feared — his wife.   And so I continued on my way to the sale.

As I passed through the gates of the château,
the rasping voice of the lean-jawed auctioneer
reached my ears as he harangued in the drizzling
rain before the steps of the château the group of
peasants gathered before him — widows in
rusty crêpe veils, shrewd old Norman farmers
in blue blouses looking for bargains, their carts
wheeled up on the mud-smeared lawn.   And
a few second-hand dealers from afar, in black
derbys, lifting a dirty finger to close a bid for
mahogany.

Close to this sordid crowd on the mud-
smeared lawn sat Le Gros, his heavy body sunk
in a carved and gilded arm-chair that had once
graced the boudoir of Madame de Savignac.
As I passed him, I saw that his face was purple
with drink.   He sat there the picture of insolent
ignorance, this pig of a peasant.

At times the auctioneer rallied the undecided

with coarse jokes, and the crowd roared, for
they are not burdened with delicacy, these
Norman farmers.

"*Allons! Allons!* my good ladies!" croaked
the auctioneer. "Forty sous for the lot. A
bed quilt for a princess and a magnificent water
filter de luxe that will keep your children well
out of the doctor's hands. *Allons!* forty sous,
forty-one — two?"

A merchant in hogs raised his red, puffy hand,
then turned away with a leer as the shrill voice
of a fisher woman cried, "Forty-five."

"Sold!" yelped the auctioneer — "sold to
madame the widow Dupuis of Hirondelette,"
who was now elbowing her broad way through
the crowd to her bargain which she struggled
out with, red and perspiring, to the mud-smeared
lawn, where her eldest daughter shrewdly exam-
ined the bedquilt for holes.

I turned away when it was all over and
followed the crowd out through the gates. Le
Gros was climbing into his cart. He was drunk
and swearing over the poor result of the sale.
De Savignac was still in his debt — and I con-

tinued on my way home, feeling as if I had attended an execution.

Half an hour later the sharp bark of my yellow puppy greeted me from beyond my wall. As I entered my courtyard, he came to me wriggling with joy. Suddenly I stopped, for my ear caught the sound of a tail gently patting the straw in the cavernous old stable beyond my spaniel's kennel. I looked in and saw a pair of eyes gleaming like opals in the gloom. Then the tawny body of Mirza, the mother, rose from the straw and came slowly and apologetically toward me with her head lowered.

"Suzette!" I called, "how did she get here?"

"The boy of Monsieur de Savignac brought her an hour ago, monsieur," answered the little maid. "There is a note for monsieur. I have left it on the table."

I went in, lighted the fire, and read the following:

"THE GARÇONNIÈRE, *Saturday*.

"Take her, my friend. I can no longer keep her with me. You have the son, it is only

right you should have the mother. We leave
for Paris to-morrow. We shall meet there soon,
I trust. If you come here, do not bring her
with you. I said good-bye to her this morning.

"JACQUES DE SAVIGNAC."

It was all clear to me now — pitifully clear —
the garçonnière had gone with the rest.

On one of my flying trips to Paris I looked
them up in their refuge, in a slit of a street.
Here they had managed to live by the strictest
economy, in a plain little nest under the roof,
composed of two rooms and a closet for a
kitchen.

One night, early in June, after some per-
suasion, I forced him to go with me to one of
those sparkling *risquée* little comedies at the
Palais Royal which he loved, and so on to
supper at the Café de la Paix, where that great
gipsy, Boldi, warms the heart with his fiddle.

The opera was just out, when we reached
our table, close to the band. Beauty and the
Beast were arriving, and wraps of sheen and

lace were being slipped from fair shoulders
into the fat waiting hands of the garçons, while
the busy maître d'hôtel beamed with his nightly
smile and jotted down the orders.

The snug supper room glittered with light,
clean linen and shining glass. Now that the
theatres were out, it had become awake with
the chatter with which these little midnight
suppers begin — suppers that so often end in
confidences, jealousy and even tears, that need
only the merriest tone of a gipsy's fiddle to
turn to laughter.

Boldi is an expert at this. He watches those
to whom he plays, singling out the one who
needs his fiddle most, and to-night he was
watching de Savignac.

We had finished our steaming dish of lobster,
smothered in a spiced sauce that makes a cold
dry wine only half quench one's thirst, and were
proceeding with a crisp salad when Boldi, with
a rushing crescendo slipped into a delicious
waltz. De Savignac now sat with his chin
sunk heavily in his hands, drinking in the melody
with its spirited accompaniment as the cym·

ballist's flexible hammers flew over the resonant
strings, the violins following the master in the
red coat, with that keen alertness with which
all real gipsies play.   I realized now, what
the playing of a gipsy meant to him.   By the
end of the waltz De Savignac's eyes were
shining.

Boldi turned to our table and bowed.

"Play," said I, to him in my poor Hungarian
(that de Savignac might not understand, for
I wished to surprise him) "a real czardas of
your people — ah! I have it!" I exclaimed.
"Play the legend and the mad dance that follows — the one that Racz Laczi loved — the
legend of the young man who went up the mountain and met the girl who jilted him."

Boldi nodded his head and grinned with
savage enthusiasm.   He drew his bow across
the sobbing strings and the legend began.
Under the spell of his violin, the chatter of the
supper room ceased — the air now heavy with
the mingled scent of perfume and cigars, seemed
to pulsate under the throb of the wild melody —
as he played on, no one spoke — the men even

forgetting to smoke; the women listening, breathing with parted lips. I turned to look at de Savignac — he was drunk and there was a strange glitter in his eyes, his cheeks flushed to a dull crimson, but not from wine.

Boldi's violin talked — now and then it wept under the vibrant grip of the master, who dominated it until it dominated those to whom it played.

The young man in the legend was rushing up the mountain path in earnest now, for he had seen ahead of him the girl he loved — now the melody swept on through the wooing and the breaking of her promise, and now came the rush of the young man down to the nearest village to drown his chagrin and forget her in the mad dance, the "Czardas," which followed.

As the czardas quickened until its pace reached the speed of a whirlwind, de Savignac suddenly staggered to his feet — his breath coming in short gasps.

"Sit down!" I pleaded, not liking the sudden purplish hue of his cheeks.

"Let — me — alone," he stammered, half angrily. "It — is so good — to — be alive again."

"You shall not," I whispered, my eye catching sight of a gold louis between his fingers. "You don't know what you are doing — it is not right — this is my dinner, old friend — *all of it*, do you understand?"

"Let — me — alone," he breathed hoarsely, as I tried to get hold of the coin — "it is my last — my last — my last!" — and he tossed the gold piece to the band. It fell squarely on the cymballum and rolled under the strings.

"Bravo!" cried a little woman opposite, clapping her warm, jewelled hands. Then she screamed, for she saw Monsieur de Savignac sway heavily, and sink back in his seat, his chin on his chest, his eyes closed.

I ripped open his collar and shirt to give him breath. Twice his chest gave a great bound, and he murmured something I did not catch — then he sank back in my arms — dead.

During the horror and grim reality of it all —
the screaming women, the physician working
desperately, although he knew all hope was
gone — while the calm police questioned me
as to his identity and domicile, I shook from
head to foot — and yet the worst was still to
come — I had to tell Madame de Savignac.

CHAPTER NINE

THE MAN WITH THE GUN

IT IS at last decided! The kind and sympathetic Minister of Agriculture has signed the official document opening the shooting-season for hares and partridges in *La belle France*, to-morrow, Sunday, the thirtieth of September. Thrice happy hunters! — they who had begun to grumble in their cafés over the rumour that the opening of the shooting-season might be postponed until the second or even third Sunday in October.

My good friend the mayor of Pont du Sable has just handed me my hunting-permit for the coming year bearing the stamp of the *République Française*, the seal of the prefecture, the signature of the préfet, and including everything, from the colour of my hair and complexion to my height, age, birth and domicile. On the back of this important piece of paper I read as follows:

That the permit must be produced at the demand of all agents authorized by law. That it is prohibited to shoot without it, or upon lands without the consent of the proprietor having the right — or outside of the season fixed by the laws of the préfets.

Furthermore:

The father — the mother — the tutor — the masters, and guardians are civilly responsible for the misdemeanours committed while shooting by their infants — wards — pupils, or domestics living with them.

And finally:

That the hunter who has lost his permit cannot resume again the exercise of the hunt until he has obtained and paid for a new one, twenty-eight francs and sixty centimes.

To-morrow, then, the jolly season opens. "*Vive la République!*"

It is a season, too, of crisp twilights after brilliant days, so short that my lost village is

plunged in darkness as early as seven, and goes
to bed to save the candle — the hour when the
grocer's light gleaming ahead of me across the
slovenly little public square becomes the only
beacon in the village; and, guided by it, I pick
my way in the dark along the narrow thoroughfare, stumbling over the laziest of the village
dogs sprawled here and there in the road outside
the doorways of the fishermen.

Across one of these thresholds I catch a
glimpse to-night of a tired fisher girl stretched
on her bed after her long day at sea.   Beside
the bed a very old woman in a white cotton
cap bends over her bowl of soup by the wavering light of a tallow dip.

"*Bonsoir*, monsieur!" croaks a hoarse voice
from the dark.   It is Marianne.   She has
fished late.

At seven-thirty the toy train rumbles into
Pont du Sable, stops for a barefooted passenger,
and rumbles out again through the village —
crawling lest it send one of the laziest dogs
yelping to its home.   The headlight on the
squat locomotive floods the way ahead, suddenly

illumining the figure of a blinking old man laden with nets and three barelegged children who scream, "*Bonsoir*, monsieur," to the engineer.

What glorious old days are these! The wealth of hedged fields — the lush green grass, white with hoar frost at daybreak — the groups of mild-eyed cows and taciturn young bulls; in all this brilliant clearness of sea air, sunshine and Norman country spreading its richness down to the very edge of the sea, there comes to the man with the gun a sane exhilaration — he is alive.

On calm nights the air is pungent and warm with the perfume of tons of apples lying heaped in the orchards, ready for the cider-making, nights, when the owls hoot dismally under a silver moon.

When the wind veers to the north it grows cold. On such nights as these "the Essence of Selfishness" seeks my fireside.

She is better fed than many other children in the lost village beyond my wall. And spoiled! — *mon Dieu!* She is getting to be hopeless.

Ah, you queen of studied cruelty and indifference! You, with your nose of coral pink,

your velvet ears that twitch in your dreams,
and your blue-white breast! You, who since
yesterday morning have gnawed to death two
helpless little birds in my hedge which you
still think I have not discovered! And yet I
still continue to feed you by hand piecemeal
since you disdain to dine from my best china,
and Suzette takes care of you like a nurse.

Eh bien! Some day, do you hear, I shall
sell you to the rabbit-skin man, who has a hook
for a hand, and the rest of you will find its way
to some cheap table d'hôte, where you will pass
as ragout of rabbit Henri IV. under a thick
sauce. What would you do, I should like to
know, if you were the vagabond cat who lives
back in the orchard, and whose four children
sleep in the hollow trunk of the tree and are content with what their mother brings them, whether
it be plain mole or the best of grasshopper.
Eh, mademoiselle? Open those topaz eyes of
yours — Suzette is coming to put you to bed.

The trim little maid entered, crossed noiselessly in the firelight to my chair, and, laying
a sealed note from my friend the Baron beneath

the lamp, picked up the sleepy cat and carried her off to her room.

The note was a delightful surprise.

"*Cher monsieur:* Will you make me the pleasure and the honour to come and do the *ouverture* of the hunt at my château to-morrow, Sunday — my auto will call for you about six of the morning. We will be about ten guns, and I count on the amiability of my partridges and my hares to make you pass a beautiful and good day. Will you accept, dear sir, the assurance of my sentiments the most distinguished?"

It was nice of the Baron to think of me, for I had made his acquaintance but recently at one of Tanrade's dinners, during which, I recall, the Baron declared to me as he lifted his left eyebrow over his cognac, that the hunt — *la chasse* — "was always amusing, and a great blessing to men, since it created the appetite of the wolf and was an excuse to get rid of the ladies." He told me, too, as he adjusted his monocle safely in the corner of his aristocratic aquiline nose, that his favourite saint was St. Hubert. He would have liked to have known

him — he must have been a *bon garçon,* this
patron saint of hunting.

"Ah! *Les femmes!"* he sighed, as he straightened his erect torso, that had withstood so many
Parisian years, against the back of his chair.
"Ah! *Les femmes!* But in zee fields zey cannot follow us? *Hein?"* He laughed, lapsing
into his broken English. "Zey cannot follow
us through zee hedges, ovaire zee rough grounds,
in zee rains, in zee muds. Nevaire take a
woman hunting," he counselled me sotto voce
beneath his vibrant hand, for Alice de Bréville
was present. "One can *nevaire* make love and
kill zee agile little game at zee same time. *Par
exemple!* You whispaire somezing in madame's
leetle ear and brrrh! a partridge — *que voulez-
vous, mon cher?"* he concluded, with a shrug.
"It is quite impossible — *quite* impossible."

I told him leisurely, as we sipped our liqueur,
of the hunting in my own country, of the lonely
tramps in the wilderness following a line of traps
in the deep snow, the blind trails, the pork
sandwich melted against the doughnuts at noon,
leaking lean-tos, smoky fires, and bad coffee.

"*Parbleu!*" he roared. "You have not zee rendezvous? You have not zee hunting breakfast? I should be quite ill — you hunt like zee Arabs — like zee gipsies — ah, yes, I forget — zee warm sandwich and zee native nuts."

He tapped the table gently with his rings, smiling the while reminiscently into his glass, then, turning again to me, added seriously:

"It is not all zee play — zee hunt. I have had zee legs broken by zee fatigue. Zee good breakfast is what you say 'indispensable' to break zee day. Zee good stories, zee camaraderie, zee good kind wine — *enfin tout!* But" — and again he leaned nearer — "but *not zee* ladies — *nevaire* — only zee memories."

I repeat, it was nice of the Baron to think of me. I could easily picture to myself as I reread his note his superb estate, that stronghold of his ancestors; the hearty welcome at its gates; the gamekeepers in their green fustians; the pairs of perfectly trained dogs; the abundance of partridges and hares; and the breakfast in the old château, a feast that would be replete with wit and old Burgundy. How

splendid are these Norman autumns! What
exhilarating old days during this season of dropping apples, blue skies, and falling leaves!
Days when the fat little French partridges
nestle in companies in the fields, shorn to stubble
after the harvest, and sleek hares at sunrise
lift their long ears cautiously above the dew-
bejeweled cobwebs along the ditches to make
sure that the green feeding-patch beyond is
safe from the man and the gun.

Fat, garrulous Monsieur Toupin of the village
becomes under the spell of Madame Vinet's best
cognac so uproarious when he has killed one
of these sleek, strong-limbed hares, that madame
is obliged to draw the turkey-red curtain over
the window of her small café that Monsieur
Toupin may not be seen by his neighbours.

"Suzette," I called, "my candle! I must
get a good night's sleep, for to-morrow I shoot
with the Baron."

"*Tiens!*" exclaimed the little maid. "At
the grand château?" And her frank eyes
opened wide. "Ah, *mais* — but monsieur will
not have to work hard for a partridge there."

"And so you know the château, my little one?"

"Ah, *mais oui*, monsieur! Is it not at La Sapinière near Les Roses? My grandfather was gardener there when I was little. I passed the château once with my mother and heard the guns back of the great wall. Monsieur will be content — ah, *mais oui!*"

"My coffee at five-thirty promptly, *ma petite!*"

"*Bien*, monsieur." And Suzette passed me my lighted candle, the flame of which rose brilliantly from its wick.

"That means good luck, monsieur," said she, pointing to the candle-flame, as my foot touched the winding stairs.

"Nonsense!" I laughed, for I am always amused at her peasant belief in superstitions. Once, I remember, I was obliged to send for the doctor — Suzette had broken a mirror.

"Ah, *mais si*," declared Suzette, with conviction, as she unlatched her kitchen door. "When the wick burns like *that* — ah, *ça!*" And with a cheery *bonsoir* she closed the door behind her.

I had just swallowed my coffee when the siren of the Baron's automobile emitted a high, devilish wail, and subsided into a low moan outside my wall. The next instant the gate of the court flew open, and I rushed out, to greet, to my surprise, Tanrade in his shooting-togs, and — could it be true? Monsieur le Curé.

"You, too?" I exclaimed in delight.

"Yes," he smiled and added, with a wink: "I could not refuse so gamy an invitation."

"And I would not let him," added Tanrade. "Quick! Where are your traps? We have a good forty kilometres ahead of us; we must not keep the Baron waiting." And the composer of ballets rushed into the house and shouldered my valise containing a dry change.

"You shall have enough partridges to fill your larder for a month," I heard him tell Suzette, and he did not forget to pat her rosy cheek in passing. Suzette laughed and struggled by him, her firm young arms hugging my gun and shell-case.

Before I could stop him, the curé, in his black soutane, had clambered nimbly to the

roof of the big car and was lashing my traps
next to Tanrade's and his own. At this instant I started to take a long breath of pure
morning air — and hesitated, then I caught the
alert eye of the chauffeur, who was grinning.

"What are you burning? Fish oil?" said I.

"*Mon Dieu*, monsieur ——" began the chauffeur.

"Cheese," called down the curé, pointing
to a round paper parcel on the roof of the
limousine. "Tanrade got it at daylight; woke
up the whole village getting it."

"Had to," explained Tanrade, as Suzette
helped him into his great coat. "The Baron
is out of cheese; he added a postscript to my
invitation praying that I would be amiable
enough to bring one. *Eh voilà!* There it is,
and real cheese at that. Come, get in, quick!"
And he opened the door of the limousine, the
interior of which was lined in gray suède and
appointed with the daintiest of feminine luxuries.

"Look out for that row of gold bottles back
of you, you brute of a farmer!" Tanrade coun-
seled me, as the curé found his seat. "If you

scratch those monograms the Baroness will never forgive you."

Then, with a wave to Suzette, we swept away from my house by the marsh, were hurled through Pont du Sable, and shot out of its narrowest end into the fresh green country beyond.

It was so thoroughly chic and Parisian, this limousine. Only a few days ago it had been shopping along the Rue de la Paix, and later rushing to the cool Bois de Boulogne carrying a gracious woman to dinner; now it held two vagabonds and a curé. We tore on while we talked enthusiastically of the day's shooting in store for us. The curé was in his best humour. How he does love to shoot and what a rattling good shot he is! Neither Tanrade nor myself, and we have shot with him day in and day out on the marsh and during rough nights in his gabion, has ever beaten him.

On we flew, past the hamlet of Fourche-la-Ville, past Javonne, past Les Roses. *Sacristi!* I thought, what if the gasoline gave out or the spark refused to sparkle, what if they had ——

Why worry? That cheese was strong enough to have gotten us anywhere.

Suddenly we slowed down, hastily consulted a blue iron sign at the crossroad, and swung briskly to the right.

A noble forest and the roofs and *tourelles* of the château now loomed ahead of us. We turned into a clean, straight road, flanked by superb oaks leading to an ancient stone gateway. A final wail from the siren, the gates swung open, and we came to a dead stop in front of the Baron, four setter dogs, and a group of gentlemen immaculately attired for the hunt. From their tan-leather leggings to their yellow dogskin gloves and gleaming guns, they were faultless.

While the Baron greeted us, his guests stood waiting to be presented; their formal bow would have done credit to a foreign embassy during an imperial audience. The next moment we were talking as naturally together and with as much camaraderie as if we had known each other for years.

"Make yourselves at home, my children!"

cried the Baron. "*Vous êtes chez vous;* the ladies have gone to Paris."

It was not such a very grand place, this estate of the Baron, after all. It had an air about it of having seen better days, but the host was a good fellow, and his welcome genuine, and we were all happy to be there. No keepers in green fustians, no array of thoroughbred dogs, but instead four plain setters with a touch of shepherd in them. The château itself was plain and comfortable within and scarred by age without. Some of the little towers had lost their tops, and the extensive wall enclosing the snug forest bulged dangerously in places.

"You will see," explained the Baron to me in his fluent French, as our little party sauntered out into the open fields to shoot, "I do not get along very well with my farmer. I must tell you this in case he gives us trouble to-day. He has the right, owing to a stupid lease my aged aunt was unwise enough to sign with him some years ago, to exclude us from hunting over many fields contiguous to my own; above all, we cannot put foot in his harvest."

"I see," I returned, with a touch of disappointment, for I knew the birds were where the harvest was still uncut.

"There are acres of grain going to seed beyond us which he would rather lose than have me hunt over," the Baron confessed. "Bah! We shall see what the *canaille* will do, for only this morning he sent me word threatening to break up the hunt. Nothing would please him better than have us all served with a *procès-verbal* for trespassing."

I confess I was not anxious to be hauled before the court of the country-seat time after time during a trial conducted at a snail's pace and be relieved of several hundred francs, for this is what a *procès-verbal* meant. It was easily seen that the Baron was in a no more tranquil state of mind himself.

"You are all my guests!" he exclaimed, with sudden heat. "That *sacré* individual will deal with *me*. It is *I* who am alone responsible," he generously added. "Ah! We shall see. If you meet him, don't let him bulldoze you. Don't show him your hunting permit if he

demands it, for what he will want is your name.
I have explained all this to the rest."

"*Eh bien!* my dear friends," he called back
to the others as we reached a cross-road, "we
shall begin shooting here.   Half of you to the
right — half to the left!"

"What is the name of your farmer?"   I
inquired, as we spread out into two slowly
moving companies.

"Le Bour," returned the Baron grimly as
the breech of his gun snapped shut.

The vast cultivated plain undulating below
us looked like the patchwork-quilt of a giantess,
stitched together with well-knit hedges.   There
were rectangles of apple-green clover, canary-
yellow squares of mustard, green pastures of ochre
stubble, rich green strips of beets, and rolling
areas of brown-ribbed furrows freshly plowed.

Time after time we were obliged to pass
around companies of partridges that had taken
refuge under the idiotic lease of the aged aunt.
It was exasperating, for, from the beginning
of the shoot, every bird seemed to know where
it was safe from the gleaming guns held so

skilfully by the *messieurs* in the yellow dogskin gloves. By eleven o'clock there were barely a score of birds in the game-bags when there should have been a hundred.

At the second cross road, the right and left party convened. It was what Le Bour had been waiting for.

A sour old man in a blue blouse now rose up out of a hedge in which he had hidden himself, and came glowering toward us. As he drew nearer I saw that his gun swung loosely in his hand and was at full cock, its muzzle wavering unpleasantly over us as he strode on. His mean old eyes glittered with rage, his jaw trembled under a string of oaths. His manner was that of a sullen bull about to charge.

There was no mistaking his identity — it was Le Bour.

"*Procès-verbal* for all of you," he bellowed; "you, Monsieur le Baron, and you, Monsieur le Vicomte," he snapped, as the Baron advanced to defend his guests. "I saw you cross my buckwheat," he declared pointing an ugly finger at the Vicomte.

"You lie!" shouted the Baron, before the Vicomte could find his words. "I forbid you to open your head to my guests. Not one of these gentlemen has set foot in your harvest. What right have *you* to carry a gun ? Where is your hunting permit ?" thundered the Baron. "Where's your commission as guard, that you should have the insolence to threaten us with a *procès-verbal*.

"Ah!" exclaimed the Baron, as the permit was not forthcoming, "I thought as much. I appoint you witness, Monsieur le Curé, the fellow has no permit." And we swelled the merriment with a forced sputter of ridicule.

"Come, my friends, we shall leave this imbecile to himself," laughed the Baron.

Le Bour sprang past him and confronted us.

"*Eh ben*, my fine gentlemen," he snarled, "you'll not get away so easily. I demand, in the name of the law, your hunting permits. Come, *allons!* All of you!"

At the same instant he tore open his blouse and displayed, to our dismay, an oval brass plaque bearing his name and the number 1247.

"There!" cried the old man, white and

trembling with rage. "There's my full commission as guard."

My companion with the gloves next to me fidgeted nervously and coughed. I saw the Vicomte turn a little pale. Tanrade shrugged his shoulders. Monsieur le Curé's face wore an expression of dignified gravity. Not once, however, had Le Bour's eyes met his own. It was evident that he reverently excluded the curé from the affair.

The Vicomte looked uncomfortable enough. The truth was, he was not known to be at the hunt. The Vicomtesse was shrewd when it came to the question of his whereabouts. A *procès-verbal* meant publicity; naturally the Vicomtesse would know. It might even reach the adorable ears of Mademoiselle Rosalie, of the *corps de ballet*, who imagined the Vicomte safe with his family. The Baron was fuming, but he did not speak.

"Your permits!" reiterated Le Bour, flourishing his license.

There was an awkward silence; not a few in the party had left their permits at home.

"*Pouf!*" exclaimed the Baron. "Enough of this! *En route*, my friends!"

"*Eh, bien!*" growled the farmer. "You refuse to produce your permits on demand of a guard. It shall be stated," he threatened, "in the *procès-verbal*." Then Le Bour turned on his muddy heel and launched a parting volley at the Baron denouncing his château and everything connected with him.

"Do not forget the time you stole the ducks of my uncle," cried the Baron, shaking a clenched fist at the old man, "or the morning — " But his words were lost on Le Bour, who had disappeared in the hedge.

By eleven-thirty we had killed some two dozen birds and three hares; and as we were now stricken with "the appetite of the wolf," we turned back to the château for breakfast.

Here a sponge and a rub-down sent us in gay spirits down to the billiard-room, where a bottle of port was in waiting — a rare bottle for particular occasions. It was "the last of a dozen," explained the Baron as we touched glasses, sent to the château by Napoleon in payment for a night's lodging during one of his campaigns. "The very time, in fact," he added, "when the little towers lost their tops."

Under the spell of the Emperor's port the Vicomte regained his nerves, and even the unpleasant incident of the morning was half forgotten while the piano in the historic salon rang merrily under Tanrade's touch until we filed in to luncheon.

It was as every French shooting-luncheon is intended to be — a pleasant little fête full of good cheer and understanding; the good soup, the decanters of Burgundy, the clean red-and-white checkered napkins and cloth, the heavy family silver, the noiseless old servants — and what an appetite we had! What a *soufflé* of potatoes, and such chicken smothered in cream! And always the "good kind wine," until the famous cheese that Tanrade had waked up Pont du Sable in procuring was passed quickly and went out to the pantry, never to return. Ah, yes! And the warm champagne without which no French breakfast is complete.

Over the coffee and liqueurs, the talk ran naturally to gallantry.

"Ah, *les femmes!* The memories," as the Baron had said.

"You should have seen Babette Deslys five years ago," remarked one of our jolly company when the Baron had left the room in search of some milder cigars.

I saw the Vicomte raise his eyebrows in subtle warning to the speaker, who, like myself, knew the Baron but slightly. If he was treading upon delicate ground he was unconscious of it, this *bon vivant* of a Parisian; for he continued rapidly in his enthusiasm, despite a second hopeless attempt of the Vicomte to check him.

"You should have seen Babette in the burlesque as Phryne at the Variétés — *une merveille, mon cher!*" he exclaimed, addressing the sous-lieutenant on his right, and he blew a kiss to the ceiling. "The complexion of a rosebud and amusing! Ah — la! la!"

"I hear her debts ran close to a million," returned the lieutenant.

"She was feather-brained," continued the

bon vivant, with a blasé shrug. "She was a good little quail with more heart than head! Poor Babette!"

"Take care!" cautioned the Vicomte point-blank, as the Baron re-entered with the box of milder Havanas.

And thus the talk ran on among these men of the world who knew Paris as well as their pockets; and so many Babettes and Francines and other careless little celebrities whose beauty and extravagance had turned peace and tranquillity into ruin and chaos.

At last the jolly breakfast came to an end. We rose, recovered our guns from the billiard-table, and with fresh courage went forth again into the fields to shoot until sunset. During the afternoon we again saw Le Bour, but he kept at a safe distance watching our movements with muttered oaths and a vengeful eye, while we added some twenty-odd partridges to the morning's score.

Toward the end of the afternoon, a week later, at Pont du Sable, Tanrade and the curé sat smoking under my sketching-umbrella on the marsh. The curé is far from a bad painter. His unfinished sketch of the distant strip of sea and dunes lay at my feet as I worked on my own canvas while the sunset lasted.

Tanrade was busy between puffs of his pipe in transposing various passages in his latest score. Now and then he would hesitate, finger the carefully thought out bar on his knee, and again his stub of a pencil would fly on through a maze of hieroglyphics that were to the curé and myself wholly unintelligible.

Suddenly the curé looked up, his keen gaze rivetted upon two dots of figures on bicycles speeding rapidly toward us along the path skirting the marsh.

"Hello!" exclaimed the curé, and he gave a low whistle. "The gendarmes!"

There was no mistaking their identity; their gold stripes and white duck trousers appeared distinctly against the tawny marsh.

The next moment they dismounted, left their wheels on the path, and came slowly across the desert of wire-grass toward us.

"*Diable!*" muttered Tanrade, under his

breath, and instantly our minds reverted to
Le Bour.

The two officials of the law were before us.

"We regret to disturb you, messieurs," began
the taller of the two pleasantly as he extracted a
note-book from a leather case next to his revolver.
"But"—and he shrugged his military shoulders
—"it is for the little affair at Hirondelette."

"Which one of us is elected?" asked Tanrade
grimly.

"Ah! *Bon Dieu!*" returned the tall one;
half apologetically. "A *procès-verbal* unfortu-
nately for you, Monsieur Tanrade. Read the
charge," he said to the short one, who had now
unfolded a paper, cleared his throat, and began
to read in a monotonous tone.

"Monsieur Gaston Emile Le Bour, agri-
culturist at Hirondelette, charges Monsieur
Charles Louis Ernest Tanrade, born in Paris,
soldier of the Thirteenth Infantry, musician,
composer, with flagrant trespass in his
buckwheat on hectare number seven, armed
with the gun of percussion on the thirtieth of
September at ten-forty-five in the morning."

"I was *not* in his *sacré* buckwheat!" declared Tanrade, and he described the entire incident of the morning.

"Take monsieur's denial in detail," commanded the tall one.

His companion produced a small bottle of ink and began to write slowly with a scratchy pen, while we stood in silence.

"Kindly add your signature, monsieur," said the tall one, when the bottle was again recorked.

Tanrade signed.

The gendarmes gravely saluted and were about to withdraw when Tanrade asked if he was "the only unfortunate on the list."

"Ah, *non!*" confessed the tall one. "There is a similar charge against Monsieur le Vicomte — we have just called upon him. Also against Monsieur le Baron."

"And what did they say?"

"*Eh bien*, monsieur, a general denial, just as monsieur has made."

"The affair is ridiculous," exclaimed Tanrade hotly.

"That must be seen," returned the tall one firmly.

Again we all saluted and they left us, recovered their bicycles, and went spinning off back to Pont du Sable.

"*Nom d'un chien!*" muttered Tanrade, while the curé and I stared thoughtfully at a clump of grass.

"Why didn't he get me?" I ventured, after a moment.

"Foreigner," explained Tanrade. "You're in luck, old boy — no record of identity, and how the devil do you suppose Le Bour could pronounce your name?"

Half an hour later I found the Vicomte, who lived close to our village. He was pacing up and down his salon in a rage.

"I was *not* in the buckwheat!" he declared frantically. "Do you suppose I have nothing better to do, my friend, than see this wretched business out at the county-seat? The Vicomtess is furious. We were to leave, for a little voyage in Italy, next week. Ah, that young son of the Baron! He is the devil! *He* is responsible for this — naturally." And he fell again to pacing the room.

I looked blankly at the Vicomte.

"Son? What young son?" I asked.

The Vicomte stopped, with a gesture of surprise.

"Ah! *Sapristi!* You do not know?" he exclaimed. "You do not know that Babette Deslys is Le Bour's daughter? That the Baron's son ran away with her and a hundred thousand francs? That the hundred thousand francs belonged to Le Bour? *Sapristi!* You did not know *that?*"

CHAPTER TEN

THE BELLS OF PONT DU SABLE

THE big yellow car came ripping down the road — a clean hard ribbon of a road skirting the tawny marsh that lay this sparkling August morning under a glaze of turquoise blue water at high tide.

With a devilish wail from its siren, the yellow car whizzed past my house abandoned by the marsh. I was just in time, as I raised my head above the rambling wall of my courtyard, to catch sight of my good friend the curé on the back seat, holding on tight to his saucer-like hat. In the same rapid glance I saw the fluttering ends of a bottle-green veil, in front of the curé's nose and knew Germaine was driving.

"Lucky curé!" I said to myself, as I returned

to my half-finished sketch, "carried off again to luncheon by one of the dearest of little women."

No wonder during his lonely winters, when every villa or château of every friend of his for miles around is closed, and my vagabond village of Pont du Sable rarely sees a Parisian, the curé longs for midsummer. It is his gayest season, since hardly a day passes but some friend kidnaps him from his presbytery that lies snug and silent back of the crumbling wall which hides both his house and his wild garden from the gaze of the passer-by.

He is the kind of curé whom it is a joy to invite — this straight, strong curé, who is French to the backbone; with his devil-may-care geniality, his irresistible smile of a comedian, his quick wit of an Irishman, and his heart of gold.

To-day Germaine had captured him and was speeding him away to a jolly luncheon of friends at her villa, some twenty kilometres below Pont du Sable — Germaine with her trim, lithe figure and merry brown eyes, eyes that can become in a flash as calm and serious as the curé's, and in turn with her moods (for Germaine is a pretty collection of moods) gleam with the impulsive devilry of a *gamine;* Germaine, who teases an old vagabond painter like myself, by daubing a purple moon in the middle of my morning sketch, adds a dab on my nose when I protest, and the next instant embraces me, and begs my forgiveness.

I cannot conceive of anyone not forgiving Germaine, beneath whose firm and delicate beauty lies her warm heart, as golden in quality as the curé's.

Ah! It is gay enough in midsummer with Germaine and such other good Bohemians as Alice de Bréville, Tanrade, and his reverence to cheer my house abandoned by the marsh.

I heard the yellow car tearing back to Pont du Sable late that night. It slowed down as it neared my walled domain, and with a wrenching grunt stopped in front of my gate. The next instant the door of my den opened and in rushed the curé.

"All of us to luncheon to-morrow at The Three Wolves! he cried, flinging his hat on

the floor; then bending, with a grin of satisfaction over the lamp chimney, he kindled the
end of a fat cigarette he had rolled in the dark.
His eyes were snapping, while the corners of
his humorous mouth twitched in a satisfied smile.   He strode up and down the room
for some moments, his hands clasped behind
him, his strong, sun-tanned face beaming in
the glow of the shaded lamplight, while he
listened to my delight over the pleasant news
he had brought.

"Ah! They are good to me, these children
of mine," he declared with enthusiasm.   "Germaine tells me there is a surprise in store for
me and that I am not to know until to-morrow,
at luncheon.   Beyond that, she would tell me
nothing, the little minx, except that I managed
to make her confess that Alice was in the secret."

He glanced at his watch, "Ah!" he ejaculated, "I must be getting to bed; you, too, my
old one, for we must get an early start in the
morning, if we are to reach The Three Wolves
by noon.   He recovered his hat from the floor,
straightened up, brushed the cigarette ashes

from the breast of his long black soutane, shiny from wear, and held out his strong hand.

"Sleep well," he counselled, "for to-morrow we shall be *en fête.*"

Then he swung open my door and passed out into the night, whistling as he crossed my courtyard a *café chantant* air that Germaine had taught him.

A moment later, the siren of the yellow car sent forth its warning wail, and he was speeding back to his presbytery under the guidance of Germaine's chauffeur.

The curé was raking out the oysters; he stood on the sandy rim of a pool of clear sea-water that lay under the noonday sun like a liquid emerald. As Monsieur le Curé plunged in his long rake and drew it back heavy with those excellent bivalves for which the restaurant at The Three Wolves has long been famous, his tall black figure, silhouetted against the distant sea and sky, reminded me of some great sea-crow fishing for its breakfast.

To the right of him crouched the restaurant,

a low wooden structure, with its back to the
breakers.   It has the appearance of being cast
there at high tide, its zigzag line of tiled roofs
drying in the air and sun, like the scaled shell
of some stranded monster of the sea.   There
is a cavernous old kitchen within, resplendent
in shining copper — a busy kitchen to-day,
sizzling in good things and pungent with the
aroma of two tender young chickens, basting
on a spit, a jolly old kitchen, far more enticing
than the dingy long dining-room adjoining it,
whose walls are frescoed in panels representing
bottle-green lobsters, gaping succulent clams,
and ferocious crabs sidling away indignantly
from nets held daintily by fine ladies and their
gallants, in costumes that were in vogue before
the revolution.   Even when it pours, this cheerless old dining-room at The Three Wolves
is deserted, since there are half a score of far
cosier little round pavilions for lovers and
intimate friends, built over the oyster pools.

Beyond them, hard by the desolate beach,
lie the rocks known as The Three Wolves.
In calm weather the surf smashes over their

glistening backs — at low water, as it happened
to be to-day, the seethe of the tide scurried
about their dripping bellies green with hairy
sea-weed.

Now and then came cheery ripples of laughter
from our little pavilion, where Germaine and
Alice de Bréville were arranging a mass of
scarlet nasturtiums, twining their green leaves
and tendrils amongst the plates of *hors d'œuvres*
and among the dust-caked bottles of Chablis
and Burgundy — Alice, whose dark hair and
olive skin are in strong contrast to Germaine's
saucy beauty.

They had banished Tanrade, who had offered
his clumsy help — and spilled the sardines. He
had climbed on the roof and dropped pebbles
down on them through the cracks and had
later begged forgiveness through the key-hole.
Now he was yelling like an Indian, this cele-
brated composer of ballets, as he swung a little
peasant maid of ten in a creaky swing beyond
the pool — a dear little maid with eyes as dark
as Alice's, who screamed from sheer delight,
and insisted on that good fellow playing all

the games that lay about them, from *tonneau*
to *bilboquet*.

Together, the curé and I carried the basket,
now plentifully filled with oysters back to the
kitchen, while Tanrade was hailed from the
pavilion, much to the little maid's despair.

"*Dépêchez-vous!*" cried Alice, who had
straightway embraced her exiled Tanrade on
his return and was now waving a summons
to the curé and myself.

"*Bon,*" shouted back the curé. "*Allons,
mes enfants, à table* — and the one who has no
appetite shall be cast into the sea — by the
heels," added his reverence.

What a breakfast followed! Such a rushing
of little maids back and forth from the jolly
kitchen with the great platters of oysters. What
a sole smothered in a mussel sauce! What a
lobster, scarlet as the cap of a cardinal and
garnished with crisp romaine! and the chickens!
and the mutton! and the *soufflé* of potatoes,
and the salad of shrimps — *Mon Dieu!* What
a luncheon, "sprayed," as the French say,
with that rare old Chablis and mellow Burgundy!

And what laughter and camaraderie went with it from the very beginning, for to be at table with friends in France is to be *en fête* — it is the hour when hearts are warmest and merriest.

Ah, you dear little women! You who know just when to give those who love you a friendly pressure of the hand, or the gift of your lips if needs be, even in the presence of so austere a personage as Monsieur le Curé. You who understand. You who are tender or merry with the mood, or contrary to the verge of exasperation — only to caress with the subtle light of your eyes and be forgiven.

It was not until we had reached our coffee and liqueur, that the surprise for the curé was forthcoming. Hardly had the tiny glasses been filled, when the clear tone of the bell ringing from the ancient church of The Three Wolves made us cease our talk to listen.

Alice turned to the curé; it was evidently the moment she had been waiting for.

"Listen," said Alice softly — "how delicious!"

"It is the bell of Ste. Marie," returned the curé.

Even Tanrade was silent now, for his reverence had made the sign of the cross. As his fingers moved I saw a peculiar look come into his eyes — a look of mingled disappointment and resignation.

Again Alice spoke: "Your cracked bell at Pont du Sable has not long to ring, my friend," she said very tenderly.

"One must be content, my child, with what one has," replied the curé.

Alice leaned towards him and whispered something in his ear, Germaine smiling the while.

I saw his reverence give a little start of surprise.

"No, no," he protested half aloud. "Not that; it is too much to ask of you with all your rehearsals at the Bouffes Parisiennes coming."

"*Parbleu!*" exclaimed Alice, "it will not be so very difficult — I shall accomplish it, you shall see what a concert we shall give — we shall make a lot of money; every one will be

there.   It has the voice of a frog, your bell.
Dieu!   What a fuss it makes over its crack.
You shall have a new one — two new ones,
mon ami, even if we have to make bigger the
belfry of your little gray church to hang them."

The curé grew quite red.   I saw for an instant
his eyes fill with tears, then with a benign smile,
he laid his hand firmly over Alice's and lifting
the tips of her fingers, kissed them twice in
gratefulness.

He was very happy.   He was happy all the
way back in Germaine's yellow car to Pont du
Sable.   Happy when he thrust his heavy key
in the rusty lock of the small door that let him
into his silent garden, cool under the stars,
and sweet with the scent of roses.

A long winter has passed since that memor-
able luncheon at The Three Wolves.   Our
little pavilion over the emerald pool will never
see us reunited, I fear.   A cloud has fallen over
my good friend the curé, a cloud so unbelievable,
and yet so dense, if it be true, and so filled with
ominous mutterings of thunder and lightning,

crime, defalcation, banishment, and the like,. that I go about my work dazed at the rumoured situation.

They tell me the curé still says mass, and when it is over, regains the presbytery by way of the back lane skirting the marsh. I am also told that he rarely even ventures into his garden,. but spends most of his days and half of his nights alone in his den with the door locked,. and strict orders to his faithful old servant Marie, who adores him, that he will see no one who calls.

For days I have not laid eyes on him — he who kept his napkin tied in a sailor's knot in my cupboard and came to breakfast, luncheon, or dinner when he pleased, waking up my house abandoned by the marsh with his good humour, joking with Suzette, my little maid-of-all-work,. until her fair cheeks grew the rosier, and rousing me out of the blues with his quick wit and his hearty laugh.

It seems impossible to me that he is guilty of what he is accused of, yet the facts seem undeniable.

Only the good go wrong, is it not so? The
bad have become so commonplace, they do not
attract our attention.

Now the ways of the curé were always just.
I have never known him to do a mean thing
in his life, far less a dishonest one. I have
known him to give the last few sous he possessed
to a hungry fisherwoman who needed bread
for herself and her brood of children and content himself with what was left among the
few remaining vegetables in his garden. There
are days, too, when he is forced to live frugally
upon a peasant soup and a pear for dinner,
and there have been occasions to my knowledge,
when the soup had to be omitted and his menu
reduced to a novel, a cigarette and the pear.

It is a serious matter, the separation of the
state from the church in France, since it has
left the priest with the munificent salary of four
hundred francs a year, out of which he must
pay his rent and give to the poor.

Once we dined nobly together upon two fat
sparrows, and again we had a blackbird for
dinner. He had killed it that morning from

his window, while shaving, for I saw the lather dried on the stock of his duck gun.

Monsieur le Curé is ingenious when it comes to hard times.

Again, there are days when he is in luck, when some generous parishioner has had the forethought to restock his larder. Upon such bountiful occasions he insists on Tanrade and myself dining with him at the presbytery as long as these luxuries last, refusing to dine with either of us until there is no more left of his own to give.

The last time I saw him, I had noticed a marked change in his reverence. He was moody and unshaven, and his saucerlike hat was as dusty and spotted as his frayed soutane. Only now and then he gave out flashes of his old geniality and even they seemed forced. I was amazed at the change in him, and yet, when I consider all I have heard since, I do not wonder much at his appearance.

Tanrade tells me (and he evidently believes it) that some fifteen hundred francs, raised by Alice's concert and paid over to the curé to

purchase the bells for his little gray church
at Pont du Sable, have disappeared and that
his reverence refuses to give any account.

Despite his hearty Bohemian spirit, Tanrade,
like most musicians, is a dreamer and as ready
as a child to believe anything and anybody.
Being a master of the pianoforte and a composer
of rare talent, he can hardly be called sane.
And yet, though I have seen him enthusiastic,
misled, moved to tears over nothing, indignant
over an imaginary insult, or ready to forgive any
one who could be fool enough to be his enemy, I
have never known him so thoroughly upset or
so positive in his convictions as when the other
morning, as I sat loafing before my fire, he
entered my den.

"It is incredible, *mon vieux*, incredible!"
he gasped, throwing himself disconsolately into
my arm-chair. "I have just been to the presbytery. Not only does he refuse to give an account
of the money, but he declines to offer any explanation beyond the one that he "spent it."
Moreover, he sits hunched up before his stove
in his little room off the kitchen, chewing the

end of a cigarette. Why, he didn't even ask me to have a drink — the curé, *mon ami* — our curé — *Mon Dieu*, what a mess! Ah, *mon Dieu!*"

He sank his chin in his hands and gazed at me with a look of utter despair.

I regarded him keenly, then I went to the decanter and poured out for him a stiff glass of applejack.

"Drink that," said I, "and get normal."

With an impetuous gesture he waved it away.

"No, not now!" he exclaimed, "wait until I tell you all — nothing until I tell you."

"Go on, then," I returned, "I want to hear all about this wretched business. Go slow and tell it to me from top to bottom. I am not as convinced of the curé's guilt as you are, old boy. There may be nothing in it more than a pack of village lies; and if there is a vestige of the truth, we may, by putting our heads together, help matters."

He started to speak, but I held up my hand.

"One thing before you proceed," I declared with conviction. "I can no more believe the

curé is dishonest than Alice or yourself. It
is ridiculous to presume so for a moment. I
have known the curé too well. He is a prince.
He has a heart as big as all outdoors. Look
at the good he's done in this village! There
is not a vagabond in it but will tell you he is
as right as rain. Ask the people he helps what
they think of him, they'll tell you 'he's just
the curé for Pont du Sable.' *Voilà!* That's
what they'll tell you, and they mean it. All
the gossip in the world can't hurt him. Here,"
I cried, forcing the glass into his hand, "get
that down you, you maker of ballets, and proceed with the horrible details, but proceed
gently, merrily, with the right sort of beat in
your heart, for the curé is as much a friend of
yours as he is of mine."

Tanrade shrugged his broad shoulders, and
for some moments sipped his glass. At length,
he set it down on the broad table at his elbow,
and said slowly: "You know how good Alice
is, how much she will do for any one she is fond
of — for a friend, I mean, like the curé. Very
well, it is not an easy thing to give a concert

in Paris that earns fifteen hundred francs for
a curé whom, it is safe to say, no one in the audience, save Germaine, Alice and myself had ever
heard of. It was a veritable *tour de force*
to organize. You were not there. I'm glad
you were not. It was a dull old concert that
would not have amused you much — Lassive
fell ill at the last moment, Delmar was in a bad
humour, and the quartet had played the night
before at a ball at the Élysée and were barely
awake. Yet in spite of it the theatre was packed;
a chic audience, too. Frambord came out with
half a column in the *Critique des Arts* with
a pretty compliment to Alice's executive energy,
and added 'that it was one of the rare soirées
of the season.' He must have been drunk when
he wrote it. I played badly — I never can
play when they gabble. It was as garrulous
as a fish market in front. *Enfin!* It was over
and we telegraphed his reverence the result;
from a money standpoint it was a '*succès fou.*'"

Tanrade leaned back and for a few seconds
gazed at the ceiling of my den.

"Where every penny has gone," he resumed,

witn a strained smile, "*Dieu sait!* There is no bell, not even the sound of one, *et voilà!*"

He turned abruptly and reached for his glass, forgetting he had drained it. A fly was buzzing on its back in the last drop. And then we both smiled grimly, for we were thinking of Monsieur le Curé.

I rang the bell of the presbytery early the next morning, by inserting my jackknife, to spare my fingers, in a loop at the end of a crooked wire which dangles over the rambling wall of the curé's garden. The door itself is of thick oak, and framed by stones overgrown with lichens — a solid old playground for nervous lizards when the sun shines, and a favourite sticking place for snails when it rains. I had to tug hard on the crooked wire before I heard a faint jingle issuing in response from the curé's cavernous kitchen, whose hooded chimney and stone-paved floor I love to paint.

Now came the klop-klop of a pair of sabots — then the creak of a heavy key as it turned over twice in the rusty lock, and his faithful Marie cautiously opened the garden door. I do not

know how old Marie is, there is so little left
of this good soul to guess by. Her small
shrunken body is bent from age and hard work.
Her hands are heavy — the fingers gnarled and
out of proportion to her gaunt thin wrists. She
has the wrinkled, leathery face of some kindly
gnome. She opened her eyes in a sort of mute
appeal as I inquired if Monsieur le Curé was
at home.

"Ah! My poor monsieur, his reverence
will see no one" — she faltered — "*Ah! Mais*"
— she sighed, knowing that I knew the change
in her master and the gossip thereof.

"My good Marie," I said, persuasively patting her bony shoulder, "tell his reverence that
I *must* see him. Old friends as we are —"

"*Bon Dieu, oui!*" she exclaimed after another
sigh. "Such old friends as you and he — I
will go and see," said she, and turned bravely
back down the path that led to his door while
I waited among the roses.

A few moments later Marie beckoned to
me from the kitchen window.

"He will see you," she whispered, as I crossed

the stone floor of the kitchen. "He is in the little room," and she pointed to a narrow door close by the big chimney, a door provided with old-fashioned little glass panes upon which are glued transparent chromos of wild ducks.

I knocked gently.

"*Entrez!*" came a tired voice from within.

I turned the knob and entered his den — a dingy little box of a room, sunk a step below the level of the kitchen, with a smoke-grimed ceiling and corners littered with dusty books and pamphlets.

He was sitting with his back to me, humped up in a worn arm-chair, before his small stove, just as Tanrade had found him. As I edged around his table — past a rack holding his guns, half-hidden under two dilapidated game bags and a bicycle tyre long out of service, he turned his hollow eyes to mine, with a look I shall long remember, and feebly grasped my outstretched hand.

"Come," said I, "you're going to get a grip on yourself, *mon ami*. You're going to get out of this wretched, unkempt state of melan-

cholia at once. Tanrade has told me much.
You know as well as I do, the village is a nest
of gossip — that they make a mountain out
of a molehill; if I were a pirate chief and had
captured this vagabond port, I'd have a few
of those wagging tongues taken out and keel-
hauled in the bay."

He started as if in pain, and again turned
his haggard eyes to mine.

"I don't believe there's a word of truth in
it," I declared hotly.

"There — *is*," he returned hoarsely, trembling so his voice faltered — "I am — a thief."

He sat bolt-upright in his chair, staring at
me like a man who had suddenly become insane.
His declaration was so sudden and amazing,
that for some moments I knew not what to
reply, then a feeling of pity took possession of
me. He was still my friend, whatever he had
done. I saw his gaze revert to the crucifix
hanging between the steel engravings of two
venerable saints, over the mantel back of the
stove — a mantel heaped with old shot bags and
empty cartridge shells.

"How the devil did it happen?" I blurted out at length. "You don't mean to say you stole the money?"

"Spent it," he replied half inaudibly.

"How spent it? On yourself?"

"No, no! Thank God — "

"How, then?"

He leaned forward, his head sunk in his hands, his eyes riveted upon mine.

"There is—so—much—dire—need of money," he said, catching his breath between his words. "We are all human — all weak in the face of another's misery. It takes a strong heart, a strong mind, a strong body to resist. There are some temptations too terrible even for a priest. I wish with all my heart that Alice had never given it into my hands."

I started to speak, but he held up his arms.

"Do not ask me more," he pleaded — "I cannot tell you — I am ill and weak — my courage is gone."

"Is there any of the money left?" I ventured quietly, after waiting in vain for him to continue.

"I do not know," he returned wearily, "most of it has gone — over there, beneath the papers, in the little drawer," he said pointing to the corner; "I kept it there. Yes, there is some left — but I have not dared count it."

Again there ensued a painful silence, while I racked my brain for a scheme that might still save the situation, bad as it looked. In the state he was in, I had not the heart to worry out of him a fuller confession. Most of the fifteen hundred francs was gone, that was plain enough. What he had done with it I could only conjecture. Had he given it to save another I wondered. Some man or woman whose very life and reputation depended upon it? Had he fallen in love hopelessly and past all reasoning? There is no man that some woman cannot make her slave. It was not many years ago, that a far more saintly priest than he eloped to Belgium with a pretty seamstress of Les Fosses. Then I thought of Germaine! — that little minx, badly in debt — perhaps? No, no, impossible! She was too clever — too honest for that.

"Have you seen Alice?" I broke our silence with at length.

He shook his head wearily. "I could not," he replied, "I know the bitterness she must feel toward me."

At that moment Marie knocked at the door. As she entered, I saw that her wrinkled face was drawn, as with lowered eyes she regarded a yellow envelope stamped with the seal of the *République Française.*

With a trembling hand she laid it beside the curé, and left the room.

The curé started, then he rose nervously to his feet, steadying himself against the table's edge as he tore open the envelope, and glanced at its contents. With a low moan he sank back in his chair.— "Go," he pleaded huskily, "I wish to be alone — I have been summoned before the mayor."

Never before in the history of the whole country about, had a curé been hauled to account. Pont du Sable was buzzing like a beehive over the affair. Along its single thoroughfare, flanked by the stone houses of the fishermen, the gossips clustered in groups. From what I caught in passing proved to me again that his reverence had more friends than enemies.

It was in the mayor's kitchen, which serves him as executive chamber as well, that the official investigation took place.

With the exception of the Municipal Council, consisting of the baker, the butcher, the grocer, and two raisers of cattle, none were to be admitted at the mayor's save Tanrade, myself and Alice de Bréville, whose presence the mayor had judged imperative, and who had been summoned from Paris.

Tanrade and I had arrived early — the mayor greeting us at the gate of his trim little garden, and ushering us to our chairs in the clean, well-worn kitchen, with as much solemnity as if there had been a death in the house. Here we sat, under the low ceiling of rough beams and waited in a funereal silence, broken only by the slow ticking of the tall clock in the corner. It was working as hard as it could, its brass pendulum swinging lazily toward three o'clock, the hour appointed for the investigation.

Monsieur le Maire to-day was no longer the genial, ruddy old raiser of cattle, who stops me whenever I pass his gate with a hearty welcome. He was all Mayor to-day, clean shaven to the raw edges of his cropped gray side-whiskers with a look of grave importance in his shrewd eyes and a firm setting of his wrinkled upper lip, that indicated the dignity of his office; a fact which was further accentuated by his carefully brushed suit of black, a clean starched collar and the tri-coloured silk sash, with gold tassels, which he is forced to gird his fat paunch with, when he either marries you or sends you to jail. The clock ticked on, its oaken case reflecting the copper light from the line of saucepans hanging beside it on the wall. Presently, the Municipal Council filed in and seated themselves about a centre table, upon which lay in readiness the official seal, pen, ink and paper. Being somewhat ill at ease in his starched shirt, the florid grocer coughed frequently, while the two cattle-raisers in their black blouses, talked in gutteral whispers over a bargain in calves. Through the open window, screened with cool vines, came the faint murmur of the village — suddenly it ceased. I rose, and going to the window, looked up the street. The curé was coming down it, striding along as straight as a savage, nodding to those who nodded to him. An old fisherwoman hobbled forth and kissed his hand. Young and old, gamblers of the sea, lifted their caps as he passed.

"The census of opinion is with him," I whispered to Tanrade, as I regained my chair. "He has his old grit with him, too."

The next instant, his reverence strode in before us — firm, cool, and so thoroughly master of himself that a feeling of intense relief stole over me.

"I have come," he said, in a clear, even voice, "in answer to your summons, Monsieur le Maire."

The mayor rose, bowed gravely, waved the curé to a chair opposite the Municipal Council, and continued in silence the closely written contents of two official documents containing the charge. The stopping of an automobile at his gate now caused him to look up significantly. Madame de Bréville had arrived. As Alice entered every man in the room rose to his feet. Never had I seen her look lovelier, gowned, as she was, in simple black, her dark hair framing her exquisite features, pale as ivory, her sensitive mouth tense as she pressed Tanrade's hand nervously, and took her seat beside us. For an instant, I saw her dark eyes flash as she met the steady gaze of the curé's.

"In the name of the *République Française*," began the mayor in measured tones.

The curé folded his arms, his eyes fixed on the open door.

"Pardon me," interrupted Alice, "I wish it to be distinctly understood before you begin, Monsieur le Maire, that I am here wholly against my will."

The curé turned sharply.

"You have summoned me," continued Alice, "and there was no alternative but to come — I know nothing in detail concerning the charge against Monsieur le Curé, nor do I wish to take any part whatever in this unfortunate affair. It is imperative that I return to Paris in time to play to-night, I beg of you that you will let me go at once."

There was a polite murmur of surprise from the Municipal Council.   The curé sprang to his feet.

"Alice, my child!" he cried, "look at me."

Her eyes met his own, her lips twitching nervously, her breast heaving.

"I wish *you* to judge me before you go," he pleaded.   "They accuse me of being a thief;" his voice rose suddenly to its full vibrant strength; "they do not know the truth."

Alice leaned forward, her lips parted.

"God only knows what this winter has been," declared his reverence — "Empty nets — always empty nets."

He struck the table with his clenched fist. "Empty nets!" he cried, "until I could bear it no longer. My children were in dire need; they came to you," he declared, turning to the mayor, "and you refused them."

The mayor shrugged his shoulders with a grunt of resentment.

"I gave what I could, while it lasted, from the public fund," he explained frankly; "there were new roads to be cut."

"Roads!" shouted the curé. "What are roads in comparison to illness and starvation? They came to me," he went on, turning to Alice, "little children — mothers, ill, with little children and not a sou in the house, and none to be earned fishing. Old men crying for bread for those whom they loved. I grew to hate the very thought of the bells; they seemed to me a needless luxury among so much misery."

His voice rose until it rang clear in the room.

"I gave it to them," he cried out. "There in my little drawer lay the power to save those who were near death from sickness, from dirt, from privation!"

Alice's ringless white hands were clenched in her lap.

"And I saw, as I gave," continued the curé, "the end of pain and of hunger — little by little I gave, hoping somehow to replace it, until I dared give no more."

He paused, and drew forth from the breast of

his soutane a small cotton sack that had once held his gun wads. "Here is what is left, gentlemen," said he, facing the Municipal Council; "I have counted it at last, four hundred and eighty francs, sixty-five centimes."

There were tears now in Alice's eyes; dark eyes that followed the curé's with a look of tenderness and pain. The mayor sat breathing irritably. As for the Municipal Council, it was evident to Tanrade and myself, that not one of these plain, red-eared citizens was eager to send a priest to jail — it was their custom occasionally to go to mass.

"Marianne's illness," continued the curé, "was an important item. You seemed to consider her case of typhoid as a malady that would cure itself if let alone. Marianne needed care, serious care, strong as she was. The girl, Yvonne, she saved from drowning last year, and her baby, she still shelters among her own children in her hut. They, too, had to be fed; for Marianne was helpless to care for them. There was the little boy, too, of the Gavons — left alone, with a case of measles well developed when I found him, on the draughty floor of a loft; the mother and father had been drunk together for three days at Bar la Rose. And there were others — the Mère Gailliard, who would have been sold out for her rent, and poor old Varnet, the fisherman; he had no home, no money, no friends; he is eighty-four years old. Most of the winter he slept in a hedge under a cast-off sail. I got him a better roof and something for his stomach, Monsieur le Maire."

He paused again, and drew out a folded paper from his pocket. "Here is a list of all I can remember I have given to, and the amounts as near as I can recall them," he declared simply. Again he turned to Alice. "It is to you, dear friend, I have come to confess," he continued; "as for you, gentlemen, my very life, the church I love, all that this village means to me, lies in your hands; I do not beg your mercy. I have sinned and I shall take the consequences — all I ask you to do is to judge fairly the error of my ways." Monsieur le Curé took his seat.

"It is for you, Madame de Bréville, to

decide," said the mayor, after some moments conference with the Council, "since the amount in question was given by your hand."

Alice rose — softly she slipped past the Municipal Council of Pont du Sable, until she stood looking up into the curé's eyes; then her arms went about his strong neck and she kissed him as tenderly as a sister.

"Child!" I heard him murmur.

"We shall give another concert," she whispered in his ear.

CHAPTER ELEVEN

THE MISER—GARRON

WE'VE had a drowning at Pont du Sable. Drownings are not infrequent on this rough Norman coast of France. Only last December five able fishermen went down within plain sight of the dunes in a roaring white sea that gave no quarter. This gale by night became a cyclone; the sea a driving hell of water, hail and screaming wind. The barometer dropped to twenty-eight. The wind blew at one hundred and twenty kilometers an hour. Six fishing boats hailing from Boulogne perished with their crews. Their women went by train to Calais, still hoping for news, and returned weeping and alone.

At Boulogne the waves burst in spray to a

height of forty feet over the breakwater —
small wonder that the transatlantic liner due
there to take on passengers, signalled to her
plunging tender already in danger— "Going
through — No passengers —" and proceeded on
her way to New York.

The sea that night killed with a blow.

This latest drowning at Pont du Sable was a
tragedy — or rather, the culmination of a series
of tragedies.

"Suicide?"

"*Non — mon ami* — wait until you hear the
whole truth of this plain tale."

On my return from shooting this morning,
Suzette brought me the news. The whole fishing village has known it since daylight.

It seems that the miser, Garron — Garron's
boy — Garron's woman, Julie, and another
woman who nobody seems to know much about,
are mixed up in the affair.

Garron's history I have known for months —
my good friend the curé confided to me much
concerning the unsavory career of this vagabond of a miser, whose hut is on the "Great

Marsh," back of Pont du Sable. Garron and I hailed "*bonjour*" to each other through the mist at dawn one morning, as I chanced to pass by his abode, a wary flight of vignon having led me a fruitless chase after them across the great marsh. At a distance through the rifts of mist I mistook this isolated hut of Garron's for a *gabion*. As I drew within hailing distance of its owner I saw that the hut stood on a point of mud and wire grass that formed the forks of the stream that snakes its way through the centre of this isolated prairie, and so on out to the open sea, two kilometers beyond.

As shrewd a rascal as Garron needed just such a place to settle on. As he returned my *bonjour*, his woman, Julie, appeared in the low doorway of the hut and grinned a greeting to me across the fork of the stream. She impressed me as being young, though she was well on in the untold forties. Her mass of fair hair — her ruddy cheeks — her blue eyes and her thick strong body, gave her the appearance of youthful buxomness.

Life must be tough enough with a man like

Garron. With the sagacity of an animal he knew the safety of the open places. By day no one could emerge from the far horizon of low woodland skirting the great marsh, without its sole inhabitant noting his approach. By night none but as clever a poacher as Garron could have found his way across the labyrinth of bogs, ditches and pitfalls. Both the hut and the woman cost Garron nothing; both were a question of abandoned wreckage.

Garron showed me his hut that morning, inviting me to cross a muddy plank as slippery as glass, with which he had spanned the stream, that he might get a closer look at me and know what manner of man I was. He did not introduce me to the woman, and I took good care, as I crossed his threshold and entered the dark living-room with its dirt floor, not to force her acquaintance, but instead, ran my eye discreetly over the objects in the gloom — a greasy table littered with dirty dishes, a bed hidden under a worn quilt and a fireplace of stones over which an iron pot of soup was simmering. Beyond was another apartment, darker than the one in which I stood — a sort of catch-all for the refuse of the former.

The whole of this disreputable shack was built of the wreckage of honest ships. It might have been torn down and reassembled into some sort of a decent craft. Part of a stout rudder with its heavy iron hinges, served as the door. For years it had guided some good ship safe into port — then the wreck occurred. For weeks after — months, perhaps — it had drifted at sea until it found a resting place on the beach and was stolen by Garron to serve him as a strong barrier.

Garron had a bad record — you saw this in his small shifty black eyes, that evaded your own when you spoke to him, and were riveted upon you the moment your back was turned. He was older than the woman — possibly fifty years of age, when I first met him, and, though he lived in the open, there was a ghastly pallor in his hard face with its determined, square jaw — a visage well seamed by sin — and crowned by a shock of black hair streaked with gray. In body he was short, with unusually

broad shoulders and unnaturally long arms.
Physically he was as strong as an ape, yet I
believe the woman could easily have strangled
him with her bare hands. Garron had been
a hard drinker in his youth, a capable thief and
a skilful poacher. His career in civilization
ended when he was young and — it is said —
good-looking.

Some twenty-five years ago — so the curé
tells me — Garron worked one summer for a
rich cattle dealer named Villette, on his farm
some sixty kilometers back of the great marsh.
Villette was one of those big, silent Normans,
who spoke only when it was worth while, and
was known for his brusqueness and his honesty.
He was a giant in build — a man whose big
hands and feet moved slowly but surely; a
man who avoided making intimate friendships
and was both proud and rich — proud of his
goods and chattels — of his vast grazing lands
and his livestock — proud too, of his big stone
farmhouse with its ancient courtyard flanked
by his stone barns and his entrance gate whose
walls were as thick as those of some feudal

stronghold; proud, too, of his wife — a plump little woman with a merry eye and whom he never suspected of being madly infatuated with his young farm hand, Garron.

Their love affair culminated in an open scandal. The woman lacked both the shrewdness and discretion of her lover; he had poached for years and had never been caught; — it is, therefore, safe to say he would as skilfully have managed to evade suspicion as far as the woman was concerned, had not things gone from bad to worse.

Villette discovered this too late; Garron had suddenly disappeared, leaving madame to weather the scandal and the divorce that followed. More than this, young Garron took with him ten thousand francs belonging to the woman, who had been fool enough to lend him her heart — a sum out of her personal fortune which, for reasons of her own, she deemed it wisest not to mention.

With ten thousand francs in bank notes next his skin, Garron took the shortest cut out of the neighbourhood. He travelled by night and slept by day, keeping to the unfrequented wood roads and trails secreted between the thick hedges, hidden by-ways that had proved their value during the guerilla warfares that were so successfully waged in Normandy generations ago. Three days later Garron passed through the modest village of Hirondelette, an unknown vagabond. He looked so poor that a priest in passing gave him ten sous.

"Courage, my son," counselled the good man — "you will get work soon. Try the farm below, they are in need of hands."

"May you never be in want, father," Garron strangled out huskily in reply. Then he slunk on to the next farm and begged his dinner. The bank notes no longer crinkled when he walked; they had taken the contour of his hairy chest. Every now and then he stopped and clutched them to see if they were safe, and twice he counted and recounted them in a di ch.

With the Great Marsh as a safe refuge in his crafty mind, he passed by the next sundown back of Pont du Sable; slept again in a hedge,

and by dawn had reached the marsh. Most
of that day he wandered over it looking for a
site for his hut. He chose the point at the forks
of the stream — no one in those days, save a
lone hunter ever came there. Moreover, there
was another safeguard. The Great Marsh
was too cut up by ditches and bogs to graze
cattle on, hence no one to tend them, and
the more complete the isolation of its sole
inhabitant.

Having decided on the point, he set about
immediately to build his hut. The sooner
housed the better, thought Garron, besides,
the packet next his chest needed a safe hiding
place.

For days the curlews, circling high above
the marsh, watched him snaking driftwood
from the beach up the crooked stream to the
point at the forks. The rope he dragged them
with he stole from a fisherman's boat picketed
for the night beyond the dunes. When he had
gathered a sufficient amount of timber he went
into Pont du Sable with three hares he had
snared and traded them for a few bare neces-

sities — an old saw, a rusty hammer and some
new nails. He worked steadily. By the end
of a fortnight he had finished the hut. When
it was done he fashioned (for he possessed
considerable skill as a carpenter) a clever hiding
place in the double wall of oak for his treasure.
Then he nailed up his door and went in search
of a mate.

He found her after dark — this girl to his
liking — at the *fête* in the neighbouring village
.of Avelot. She turned and leered at him as
he nudged her elbow, the lights from the merry-
go-round she stood watching illumining her
wealth of fair hair and her strong young figure
silhouetted against the glare. Garron had studied
her shrewdly, singling her out in the group of
village girls laughing with their sweethearts.
The girl he nudged he saw did not belong to
the village — moreover, she was barefooted,
mischievously drunk, and flushed with riding
on the wooden horses. She was barely eighteen.
She laughed outright as he gripped her strong
arm, and opened her wanton mouth wide, show-

ing her even, white teeth. In return for her
welcome he slapped her strong waist soundly.

"*Allons-y* — what do you say to a glass,
ma belle?" ventured Garron with a grin.

"*Eh ben!* I don't say no," she laughed
again, in reply.

He felt her turn instinctively toward him—
there was already something in common between
these two. He pushed her ahead of him through
the group with a certain familiar authority.
When they were free of the crowd and away
from the lights his arm went about her sturdy
neck and he crushed her warm mouth to his
own.

"*Allons-y* —" he repeated —"Come and have
a glass."

They had crossed in the mud to a dingy
tent lighted by a lantern; here they seated
themselves on a rough bench at a board table,
his arm still around her. She turned to leer
at him now, half closing her clear blue eyes.
When he had swallowed his first thimbleful of
applejack he spat, and wiped his mouth with
the back of his free hand, while the girl grew

garrulous under the warmth of the liquor and
his rough affection. Again she gave him her
lips between two wet oaths. No one paid any
attention to them — it was what a *fête* was
made for. For a while they left their glasses
and danced with the rest to the strident music
of the merry-go-round organ.

It was long after midnight when Garron
paid his score under the tent. She had told
him much in the meantime — there was no one
to care whom she followed. She told him, too,
she had come to the *fête* from a hamlet called
Les Forêts, where she had been washing for
a woman. The moon was up when they took
the highroad together, following it until it
reached the beginning of Pont du Sable, then
Garron led the way abruptly to the right up a
tangled lane that ran to an old woodroad that
he used to gain the Great Marsh. They went
lurching along together in comparative silence,
the man steadying the girl through the dark
places where the trees shut out the moon. Garron knew the road as well as his pocket — it
was a favourite with him when he did not wish

to be seen. Now and then the girl sang in a maudlin way:

> "*Entrez, entrez, messieurs,*
> *C'est l'amour qui vous attend.*"

It was gray dawn when they reached the edge of the Great Marsh that lay smothered under a blanket of chill mist.

"It is over there, my nest," muttered Garron, with a jerk of his thumb indicating the direction in which his hut lay. Again he drew her roughly to him.

"*Dis donc, toi!*" he demanded brusquely: "how do they call you?" It had not, until then, occurred to him to ask her name.

"*Eh ben* — Julie," she replied. "It's a *sacré* little name I never liked. *Eh, tu sais,*" she added slowly — "when I don't like a thing —" she drew back a little and gazed at him sullenly —"*Eh ben* — I am like that when I don't like a thing." Her flash of temper pleased him — he had had enough of the trustful kitten of Villette's.

"Come along," said he gruffly.

"*Dis donc, toi,*" she returned without moving.

"It is well understood then about my dress
and the shoes?"

"*Mais oui! Bon Dieu!*" replied the peasant
irritably. He was hungry and wanted his soup.
He swore at the chill as he led the way across
the marsh while she followed in his tracks,
satisfied with his promise of the dress and shoes.
She wanted a blue dress and she had seen the
shoes that pleased her some months before in
the grocery at Pont du Sable when a dog and
she had dragged a fisherwoman in her cart for
their board and lodging.

By the time they reached the forks of the
stream the rising sun had melted the blanket
of the mist until it lay over the desolate prairie
in thin rifts of rose vapour.

It was thus the miser, Garron, found his
mate.

Julie proved to be a fair cook, and the two
lived together, at the beginning, in comparative
peace. Although it was not until days after the
fête at Avelot that she managed to hold him to
his promise about the blue dress, he sent her

to Pont du Sable for her shoes the day after their arrival on the marsh — she bought them and they hurt her. The outcome of this was their first quarrel.

"*Sacré bon Dieu!*" he snarled — "thou art never content!" Then he struck her with the back of his clenched fist and, womanlike, she went whimpering to bed. Neither he nor she thought much of the blow. Her mind was on the shoes that did not fit.

When she was well asleep and snoring, he ran his sinewy arm in the hole he had made in the double wall — lifted the end of a short, heavy plank, caught it back against a nail and gripped the packet of bank notes that lay snug beneath it. Satisfied they were safe and his mate still asleep, he replaced the plank over his fortune — crossed the dirt floor to his barrier of a door, dropped an iron rod through two heavy staples, securely bolting it — blew out the tallow dip thrust in the neck of an empty bottle, and went to bed.

Months passed — months that were bleak and wintry enough on the marsh for even a hare to take to the timber for comfort. During most of that winter Garron peddled the skins of rabbits he snared on the marsh, and traded and bought their pelts, and he lived poor that no one might suspect his wealth. He and his mate rose, like the wild fowl, with the sun and went to bed with it, to save the light of the tallow dip. Though I have said she could easily have strangled him with her hands, she refrained. Twice, when she lay half awake she had seen him run his wiry arm in the wall — one night she had heard the lifting of the heavy plank and the faint crinkling sound of the package as he gripped it. She had long before this suspected he had money hidden.

Julie was no fool!

With the spring the marsh became more tenable. The smallest song birds from the woods flitted along the ditches; there were days, too, when the desolate prairie became soft — hazy — and inviting.

At daybreak, the beginning of one of these delicious spring days, Garron, hearing a sharp cry without, rose abruptly and unbolted his barrier.   He would have stepped out and across his threshold had not his bare foot touched something heavy and soft.   He looked down — still half asleep — then he started back in a sort of dull amazement.   The thing his foot had touched was a bundle — a rolled and well-wrapped blanket, tied with a stout string.   The sharp cry he had heard he now realized, issued from the folds of the blanket.   Garron bent over it, his thumb and forefinger uncovering the face of a baby.

"*Sacristi!*" he stammered — then leaned back heavily against the old rudder of a door. Julie heard and crawled out of bed.   She was peering over his shoulder at the bundle at his feet before he knew it.

Garron half wheeled and faced her as her breath touched his coarse ear.

"*Eh bien!* what is it?" he exclaimed, searching vainly for something else to say.

"*Eh ben! Ça! Nom de Dieu!*" returned his mate nodding to the bundle.   "It is pretty — that!"

"*Tu m'accuses, hein?*" he snarled.

"They do not leave bundles of that kind at the wrong door," she retorted in reply, half closing her blue eyes and her red hands.

"*Allons! allons!*" he exclaimed with heat, still at a loss for his words.

With her woman's instinct she brushed past him and started to pick up the bundle, but he was too quick for her and drew her roughly back, gripping her waist so sharply that he felt her wince.

"It does not pass like that!" he cried sharply. "*Eh ben!* listen to me. I'm too old a rat to be made a fool of — to be tricked like that!"

"Tricked!" she laughed back — "No, my old one — it is as simple as *bonjour,* and since it is thine thou wilt keep it. Thou'lt — keep what thou —"

The pent-up rage within him leaped to his throat:

"It does not pass like that!" he roared. With his clenched fist he struck her squarely across the mouth. He saw her sink limp to the ground, bleeding, her head buried between her knees. Then he picked up the child and started with it across the plank that spanned the fork of the stream. A moment later, still dizzy from the blow, she saw him dimly, making rapidly across the marsh toward a bend in the stream. Then the love of a mother welled up within her and she got to her feet and followed him.

"Stay where thou art!" he shouted back threateningly.

The child in his arms was screaming. She saw his hand cover its throat — the next moment she had reached him and her two hands were about his own in a grip that sent him choking to his knees. The child rolled from his arms still screaming, and the woman who was strangling Garron into obedience now sank her knee in his back until she felt him give up.

"*Assez!*" he grunted out when he could breathe.

"*Eh ben!* I am like *that* when I don't like a thing!" she cried, savagely repeating her old words. He looked up and saw a dangerous gleam in her eyes. "*Ah, mais oui alors!*" she shouted defiantly. "Since it is thine thou wilt keep it!"

Garron did not reply. She knew the fight was out of him and picked up the still screaming baby, which she hugged to her breast, crooning over it while Garron got lamely to his feet. Without another word she started back to the hut, Garron following his mate and his son in silence.

Years passed and the boy grew up on the marsh, tolerated by Garron and idolized and spoiled by Julie — years that transformed the black-eyed baby into a wiry, reckless young rascal of sixteen with all the vagabond nature of his father — straight and slim, with the clear-cut features of a gypsy. A year later the brother of Madame Villette, a well-known figure on the Paris Bourse, appeared and after a satisfactory arrangement with Garron, took the boy with him to Paris to be educated.

It was hard on Julie, who adored him. Her consent was not even asked, but at the time she consoled herself with the conviction, however, that the good fortune that had fallen to the lot of the baby she had saved, was for the best. The uncle was rich — that in itself appealed strongly to her peasant mind. That, and her secret knowledge of Garron's fortune, for she had discovered and counted it herself and, motherlike, told the boy.

In Paris the attempt to educate Jacques Baptiste Garron was an expensive experiment. When he went to bed at all it was only when the taverns and cafés along the "Boul-miche" closed before dawn. Even then he and his band of idle students found other retreats and more glasses in the all-night cafés near the Halles. And so he ate and drank and slept and made love to any little outcast who pleased him — one of these amiable *petites femmes* — the inside of whose pocketbook was well greased with rouge — became his devoted slave.

She was proud of this handsome devil-may-care "type" of hers and her jealousy was something to see to believe. Little by little she dominated him until he ran heavily in debt. She even managed the uncle when the nephew failed —

she was a shrewd little brat — small and tense
as wire, with big brown eyes and hair that was
sometimes golden and sometimes a dry Titian
red, according to her choice. Once, when she
left him for two days, Garron threatened to
kill himself.

"*Pauvre gosse!*" she said sympathizingly on
her return — and embraced him back to sanity.

The real grain of saneness left in young Garron was his inborn love of a gun. It was the
gun which brought him down from Paris, back
to the Great Marsh now and then when the
ducks were on flight.

He had his own *gabion* now at the lower end
of the bay at Pont du Sable, in which he slept
and shot from nights when the wind was northeast — a comfortable, floating box of a duck-
blind sunk in an outer jacket of tarred planks
and chained to a heavy picket driven in the mud
and wire grass, for the current ran dangerously
strong there when the tide was running
out.

Late in October young Garron left Paris
suddenly and the girl with the Titian hair was

with him. He, like his father, needed a safe
refuge. Pressed by his creditors he had forged
his uncle's name. The only way out of the
affair was to borrow from Julie to hush up the
matter. It did not occur to him at the time
how she would feel about the girl; neither did
he realize that he had grown to be an arrogant
young snob who now treated Julie, who had
saved his life, and pampered him, more like
a servant than a foster-mother.

The night young Garron arrived was at the
moment of the highest tides. The four supped
together that night in the hut — the father
silent and sullen throughout the meal and Julie
insanely jealous of the girl. Later old Garron
went off across the marsh in the moonlight to
look after his snares.

When the three were alone Julie turned to
the boy. For some moments she regarded him
shrewdly. She saw he was no longer the wild
young savage she had brought up; there was
a certain nervous, blasé feebleness about his
movements as he sat uneasily in his chair, his
hands thrust in the pockets of his hunting coat,

his chin sunk on his chest. She noticed
too, the unnatural redness of his lips and the
haggard pallor about his thin, sunken
cheeks.

"*Eh ben, mon petit* —" she began at length.
"It is a poor place to get fat in, your Paris!
They don't feed you any too well — *hein?* —
Those grand restaurants you talk so much about.
Pouf!"

"*Penses-tu?*" added the girl, since Garron did not reply. Instead he lighted a fresh
cigarette, took two long puffs from it, and threw
it on the floor.

The girl, angered at his silence and lack of
courage, gave him a vicious glance.

"*Hélas!*" sighed Julie, "you were quicker
with your tongue when you were a baby."

"*Ah zut!*" exclaimed the girl in disgust.
"He has something to tell you —" she blurted
out to Julie.

"*Eh ben!* What?" demanded Julie firmly.

"I need some money," muttered the boy
doggedly. "I *need it!*" he cried suddenly,
gaining courage in a sort of nervous hysteria.

Julie stared at him in amazement, the girl watching her like a lynx.

"*Bon Dieu!*" shouted Julie. "And it is because of *that* you sit there like a sick cat! Listen to me, my little one. Eat the good grease like the rest of us and be content if you keep out of jail."

The boy sank lower in his chair.

"It will be jail for me," he said, "unless you help me. Give me five hundred francs. I tell you I am in a bad fix. *Sacré bon Dieu!* —you *shall* give it to me!" he cried, half springing from his chair.

"Shut up, thou," whispered the girl — "not so fast!"

"Do you think it rains money here?" returned Julie, closing her red fists upon the table, "that all you have to do is to ask for it? *Ah, mais non, alors!*"

The boy slunk back in his chair staring at the tallow dip disconsolately. The girl gritted her small teeth — somehow, she felt abler than he to get it out of Julie in the end.

"You stole it, *hein?*" cried Julie, "like your

father. Name of a dog! it is the same old trick that, and it brings no good. *Allons!*" she resumed after a short pause. "*Dépêche toi!* Get out for your ducks — I'm going to bed."

"Give me four hundred," pleaded the boy.

"Not a sou!" cried Julie, bringing her fist down on the greasy table, and she shot a jealous glance at the girl.

Without a word, young Garron rose dejectedly, got into his goatskin coat, picked up his gun and, turning, beckoned to the girl.

"Go on!" she cried; "I'll come later."

"He is an infant," said she to Julie, when young Garron had closed the door behind him. "He has no courage. You know the fix we are in — the Commissaire of Police in Paris already has word of it."

Julie did not reply; she still sat with her clenched fists outstretched on the table.

"He has forged his uncle's check," snapped the girl.

Julie did not reply.

"*Ah, c'est comme ça!*" sneered the girl with

a cool laugh — "and when he is in jail," she cried aloud, "*Eh, bien—quoi?*"

"He will not have *you*, then," returned Julie faintly.

"Ah ——" she exclaimed. She slipped her tense little body into her thick automobile coat and with a contemptuous toss of her chin passed out into the night, leaving the door open.

"Jacques!" she called shrilly — "Jacques! — *Attends.*"

"*Bon!*" came his voice faintly in reply from afar on the marsh.

After some moments Julie got slowly to her feet, crossed the dirt floor of the hut and closing the door dropped the bar through the staples. Then for the space of some minutes she stood by the table struggling with a jealous rage that made her strong knees tremble. She who had saved his life, who had loved him from babyhood — she told herself — and what had he done for her in return? The great Paris that she knew nothing of had stolen him; Paris had given him *her* — that little viper with her red mouth; Paris had ruined him — had turned him into a thief like his father. Silently she cursed his uncle. Then her rage reverted again to the girl. She thought too, of her own life with Garron — of all its miserly hardships. "They have given me nothing —" she sobbed aloud — "nothing."

"Five hundred francs would save him!" she told herself. She caught her breath, then little by little again the motherly warmth stole up into her breast deadening for the moment the pain of her jealousy. She straightened to her full height, squaring her broad shoulders like a man and stepped across to the wall.

"It is as much mine as it is his," she said between her teeth.

She ran her arm into the hole in the wall, lifted the heavy plank and drew out a knitted sock tied with a stout string. From the toe she drew out Garron's fortune.

"He shall have it — the *gosse* —" she said, "and the rest — is as much mine as it is his."

She thrust the package in her breast.

Half an hour later Julie stood, scarcely breathing, her ear to the locked door of his *gabion*.

"A pretty lot you came from," she overheard the girl say, "that old cat would sooner see you go to jail." The rest of her words were half lost in the rush and suck of the tide slipping out from the *gabion's* outer jacket of boards. The heavy chain clinked taut with the pull of the outgoing tide, then relaxed in the back rush of water.

"Bah!" she heard him reply, "they are pigs, those peasants. I was a fool to have gone to them for help."

"You had better have gone to the old man," taunted the girl, "as I told you at first."

"He is made of the same miserly grizzle as she," he retorted hotly. Again the outrush of the tide drowned their words.

Julie clenched her red fists and drew a long breath. A sudden frenzy seized her. Before she realized what she was doing, she had crawled in the mud on her hands and knees to the heavy picket. Here she waited until the backward rush again slackened the chain, then she half drew the iron pin that held the last link. Half drew it! Had the girl been alone, she told herself, she would have given her to the ebb tide.

Julie rose to her feet and turned back across the marsh, unconscious that the last link was nearly free and that the jerk and pull of the outgoing tide was little by little freeing the pin from the link.

She kept on her way, towards a hidden wood road that led down to the marsh at the far end of Pont du Sable and beyond.

She was done with the locality forever. Garron's money was still in her breast.

At the first glimmer of dawn the next morning, the short, solitary figure of a man prowled the beach. He was hatless and insane with rage. In one hand he gripped an empty sock. He would halt now and then and wave his long, ape-like arms — cursing the deep strip of sea water that prevented him from crossing to the hard desert of sand beyond — far out upon which lay an upturned *gabion*. Within this

locked and stranded box lay two dead bodies.
Crabs fought their way eagerly through the
cracks of the water-sprung door, and over it,
breasting the salt breeze, slowly circled a cor-
morant — curious and amazed at so strange
a thing at low tide.

CHAPTER TWELVE

MIDWINTER FLIGHTS

ONE dines there much too well.

This snug Restaurant des Rois stands back from the grand boulevard in a slit of a street so that its ancient windows peer out askance at the gay life streaming by the corner.

The burgundy at "Les Rois" warms the soul, and the Chablis! Ah! where else in all Paris is there such Chablis? golden, sound and clear as topaz. Chablis, I hold, should be drank by some merry blonde whose heart is light; Burgundy by a brunette in a temper.

The small café on the ground floor is painted white, relieved by a frieze of gilded garlands and topped by a ceiling frescoed with rosy nymphs romping in a smoked turquoise sky.

Between five and seven o'clock these mid-winter afternoons the café is filled with its *habitués* — distinguished old Frenchmen, who sip their absinthe leisurely enough to glance over the leading articles in the conservative *Temps* or the slightly gayer *Figaro*. Upstairs, by means of a spiral stairway, is a labyrinth of narrow, low-ceiled corridors leading to half a dozen stuffy little *cabinets particuliers*, about whose faded lambrequins and green velveted chairs there still lurks the scent of perfumes once in vogue with the gallants, beaux and belles of the Second Empire.

Alice de Bréville, Tanrade, and myself, are dining to-night in one of these *intime* little rooms. The third to the left down the corridor.

Sapristi! what a change in Tanrade. He is becoming a responsible person — he has even grown neat and punctual — he who used to pound at the door of my house abandoned by the marsh at Pont du Sable, an hour late for dinner, dressed in a fisherman's sea-going overalls of brown canvas, a pair of sabots and a hat that any passing vagabond might have discarded by the roadside. I could not help noticing carefully to-night his new suit of black broadcloth, with its standing collar, buttoned up under his genial chin. His black hair is neatly combed and his broad-brimmed hat that hangs over my own on the wall, is but three days old. Thus had this *bon garçon* who had won the Prix de Rome been transformed — and Alice was responsible, I knew, for the change. Who would not change anything for so exquisite and dear a friend as Alice? She, too, was in black, without a jewel — a gown which her lithe body wore with all its sveltness — a gown that matched her dark eyes and hair, accentuating the clean-cut delicacy of her features and the ivory clearness of her olive skin. She was a very merry Alice to-night, for her long engagement at the Bouffes Parisiennes was at an end. And she had been making the best of her freedom by keeping Tanrade hard at work over the score of his new ballet. They are more in love with each other than ever — so much so that they insist on my dining with them, and so these little dinners of three at

"Les Rois" have become almost nightly occur-
rences. It is often so with those in love to be
generous to an old friend — even lovers have
need of company.

We were lingering over our coffee when the
talk reverted to the new ballet.

"It is done, *ma chérie*," declared Tanrade,
in reply to an imperative inquiry from Alice.
"Bavière shall have the whole of the second
act to-morrow."

"And the ballet in the third?" she asked
sternly, lifting her brilliant eyes.

"*Eh, voilà!*" laughed that good fellow, as
he drew forth from his pocket a thin roll of
manuscript and spread it out before her, that
she might see — but it was not discreet for me
to continue, neither is it good form to embrace
before the old *garçon de café*, who at that
moment entered apologetically with the liqueurs
— as for myself, I have long since ceased to
count in such tender moments of reward, during
which I am of no more consequence than a
faithful poodle.

Again the garçon entered, this time with

smiling assurance, for be brought me a telegram forwarded from my studio by my concierge. I opened the despatch: the next instant I jumped to my feet.

"Read!" I cried, poking the blue slip under Tanrade's nose, "it's from the curé."

"Howling northeast gale" — Tanrade read aloud — "Duck and geese — come midnight train, bring two hundred fours, one hundred double zeros for ten bore."

"*Vive le curé!*" I shouted, "the good old boy to let us know. A northeast gale at last — a howler," he says.

"He is charming — the curé," breathed Alice, her breast heaving — "Charming!" she repeated in a voice full of suppressed emotion.

Tanrade did not speak. He had let the despatch slip to the floor and sat staring at his glass.

"You'll come, of course," I said with sudden apprehension, but he only shook his head. "What! you're not going?" I exclaimed in amazement. "We'll kill fifty ducks a night — it's the gale we've been waiting for."

I saw the sullen gleam that had crept into Alice's eyes soften; she drew near him — she barely touched his arm:

"Go, *mon cher!*" she said simply — "if you wish."

He lifted his head with a grim smile, and I saw their eyes meet. I well knew what was passing in his mind — his promise to her to work — more than this, I knew he had not the heart to leave her during her well-earned rest.

"*Ah! les hommes!*" Alice exclaimed, turning to me impetuously — "you are quite crazy, you hunters."

I bowed in humble apology and again her dark eyes softened to tenderness.

"*Non* — forgive me, *mon ami*," she went on, "you are sane enough until news comes of those wretched little ducks, then, *mon Dieu!* there is no holding you. Everything else goes out of your head; you become as mad as children rushing to a fête. Is it not so?"

Still Tanrade was silent. Now and then he gave a shrug of his big shoulders and toyed with his half empty glass of liqueur. *Sapristi!* it is not easy to decide between the woman you love and a northeast gale thrashing the marsh in front of my house abandoned. He, like myself, could already picture in his mind's eye duck after duck plunge out of the night among our live decoys. My ears, like his own, were already ringing with the roar of the guns from the *gabions* — I could not resist a last appeal.

"Come," I insisted — "both of you — no — seriously — listen to me. There is plenty of dry wood in the garret; you shall have the *chambre d'amis*, dear friend, and this brute of a composer shall bunk in my room — we'll live, and shoot and be happy. Suzette will be overjoyed at your coming. Let me wire her to have breakfast ready for us?"

Alice laughed softly: "You are quite crazy, my poor friend," she said, laying her white hand on my shoulder. "You will freeze down there in that stone house of yours. Oh, la! la!" she sighed knowingly — "the leaks for the wind — the cold bedrooms, the cold stone floors — B-r-r-h-h!"

Tanrade straightened back in his chair: "No," said he, "it is impossible; Bavière can not wait. He must have his score. The rehearsals have been delayed long enough as it is — Go, *mon vieux*, and good luck to you!"

Again the old garçon entered, this time with the timetable I had sent him for in a hurry.

"*Voilà*, monsieur!" he began excitedly, his thumbnail indicating the line — "the 12.18, as monsieur sees, is an express — monsieur will not have to change at Lisieux."

"*Bon!*" I cried — "quick — a taxi-auto."

"*Bien*, monsieur — a good hunt to monsieur," and he rushed out into the narrow corridor and down the spiral stairs while I hurried into my coat and hat.

Tanrade gripped my hand:

"Shoot straight!" he counselled with a smile. Alice gave me her cheek, which I reverently kissed and murmured my apologies for my insistence in her small ear. Then I swung open the door and made for the spiral stairs. At the bottom step I stopped short. I had completely forgotten I should not return until after New Year's, and I rushed back to wish them a *Bonne Année* in advance, but I closed the door of the stuffy little *cabinet particulier* quicker than I opened it, for her arms were about the sturdy neck of a good comrade whose self-denial made me feel like the mad infant rushing to the fête.

"*Bonne Année, mes enfants!*" I called from the corridor, but they did not hear.

Ten minutes later I reached my studio, dumped three hundred cartridges into a worn valise and caught the 12.18 with four minutes to spare.

Enfin! it is winter in earnest!

The northeast gale gave, while it lasted, the best shooting the curé and I have ever had. Then the wind shifted to the southwest with a falling barometer, and the flights ceased. Again, for three days, the Norman coast has been thrashed by squalls of driving snow. The wild geese are honking in V-shaped lines to an inland refuge for the white sea is no longer tenable. Curlews cry hoarsely over the frozen fields. It is tough enough lying hidden in my sand pit on the open beach beyond the dunes, where I crack away at the ricketing flights of fat gray plover and beat myself to keep warm. Fuel is scarce and there is hardly a sou to be earned fishing in such cruel weather as this.

The country back of my house abandoned by the marsh is now stripped to bare actualities — all things are reduced to their proper size. Houses, barns and the skeletons of leafless trees stand out, naked facts in the landscape. The orchards are soggy in mud and the once green feathery lane back of my house abandoned, is now a rough gash of frozen pools and rotten leaves.

Birds twitter in the thin hedges.

I would never have believed my wild garden, once so full of mystery — gay flowers, sunshine and droning bees, to be so modest in size. A few rectangles of bare, frozen ground, and a clinging vine trembling against the old wall, is all that remains, save the scraggly little fruit trees green with moss. Beyond, in a haze of chill sea mist, lie the woodlands, long undulating ribbons of gray twigs crouching under a leaden sky.

In the cavernous cider press whose doors creak open within my courtyard Père Bordier and a boy in eartabs, are busy making cider. If you stop and listen you can hear the cider trickling into the cask and Père Bordier encouraging the patient horse who circles round and round a great stone trough in which revolve two juggernauts of wooden wheels. The place reeks with the ooze and drip of crushed apples. The giant screw of oak, the massive beams, seen dimly in the gloomy light that filters through a small barred window cut through the massive stone wall, gives the old pressoir the appearance of some feudal torture chamber. Blood ran once, and people shrieked in such places— as these.

To-morrow begins the new year and every peasant girl's cheeks are scrubbed bright and her hair neatly dressed, for to-morrow all France embraces — so the cheeks are rosy in readiness.

" *Tiens*, mademoiselle!" exclaims the butcher's boy clattering into my kitchen in his sabots.

Eh, voilà! My good little maid-of-all-work, Suzette, has been kissed by the butcher's boy and a moment later by Père Bordier, who has left the cider press for a steaming bowl of *café au lait;* and ten minutes later by the Mère Pequin who brings the milk, and then in turn by the postman — by her master, by the boy in eartabs and by every child in the village since daylight for they have entered my court-yard in droves to wish the household of my house abandoned a happy new year, and have gone away content with their little stomachs, filled and two big sous in their pockets.

And now an old fisherman enters my door. It is the Père Varnet — he who goes out with his sheep dog to dig clams, since he is eighty-four and too old to go to sea.

"*Ah, malheur!*" he sighs wearily, lifting his cap with a trembling hand as seamed and tough as his tarpaulin. "Ah, the bad luck," he repeats in a thin, husky voice. "I would not have deranged monsieur, but *bon Dieu*, I am hungry.

I have had no bread since yesterday. It is a
little beast this hunger, monsieur. There are
no clams — I have searched from the great
bank to Tocqueville."

It is surprising how quick Suzette can heat
the milk.

The old man is now seated in her kitchen
before a cold duck of the curé's killing and
hot coffee — real coffee with a stiff drink of
applejack poured into it, and there is bread
and cheese besides. Like hungry men, he eats
in silence and when he has eaten he tells me his
dog is dead — that woolly sheep dog of his with
a cast in one fishy green eye.

"*Oui*, monsieur," confided the old man, "he
is dead. He was all I had left. It is not gay,
monsieur, at eighty-four to lose one's last friend
— to have him poisoned."

"Who poisoned him?" I inquired hotly —
"was it Bonvin the butcher? They say it was
he poisoned both of Madame Vinet's cats."

"*Eh, ben!*" he returned, and I saw the tears
well up into his watery blue eyes — "one should
not accuse one's neighbours, but they say it

was he, monsieur — they say it was in his garden that Hector found the bad stuff — there are some who have no heart, monsieur."

"Bonvin!" I cried, "so it was that pig who poisoned him, eh? and you saved his little girl the time the *Belle Marie* foundered."

"*Oui*, monsieur — the time the *Belle Marie* foundered. It is true I did — we did the best we could! Had it not been for the fog and the ebb tide I think we could have saved them all."

He fell to eating again, cutting into the cheese discreetly — this fine old gentleman of the sea.

It is a pity that some one has not poisoned Bonvin I thought. A short thick fellow, is Bonvin, with cheeks as red as raw chops and small eyes that glitter with cruelty. Bonvin, whose youngest child — a male, has the look and intelligence of a veal and whose mother weighs one hundred and five kilos — a fact which Bonvin is proud of since his first wife, who died, was under weight despite the fact that the Bonvins being in the business, eat meat twice daily. I have always believed the veal infant's hair is curled in suet. Its face grows purple after meals.

A rough old place is my village of vagabonds in winter, and I am glad Alice did not come. Poor Tanrade — how he would have enjoyed that northeast gale!

Two weeks later there came to my house abandoned by the marsh such joyful news that my hand trembled as I realized it — news that made my heart beat quicker from sudden surprise and delight. As I read and reread four closely written pages from Tanrade and a corroborative postscript from Alice, leaving no doubt as to the truth.

"Suzette! Suzette!" I called. "Come quick — *Eh! Suzette!*"

I heard her trim feet running to me from the garden. The next instant she opened the door of my den and stood before me, her blue eyes and pretty mouth both open in wonder at being so hurriedly summoned.

"What is the matter, monsieur?" she

exclaimed panting, her fresh young cheeks all the rosier from her run.

"Monsieur Tanrade and Madame de Bréville are going to be married," I announced as calmly as I could.

"*Hélas!*" gasped Suzette.

"*Et voilà — et voilà!*" I cried, throwing the letter back on the table, while I squared my back to the blazing fire of my den and waited for the little maid's astonishment to subside.

Suzette did not speak.

"It is true, nevertheless," I added with enthusiasm, "they are to be married in Pont du Sable. We shall have a fête such as there never was. Ah! you will have plenty of cooking to do, *mon enfant*. Run and find Monsieur le Curé— he must know at once."

Suzette did not move — without a word she buried her face in her apron and burst into tears:

"Oh, monsieur!" she sobbed. "Oh, monsieur! It is true — that — I — I — have — no luck!"

I looked at her in astonishment.

"*Eh, bien!* my child," I returned — "and it is thus you take such happy news?"

"*Ah, mon Dieu!*" sobbed the little maid — "it is — true — I — have no luck."

"What is the matter Suzette — tell me?" I pleaded. Never had I seen her so broken-hearted, even on the day she smashed the mirror.

I saw her sway toward me like the child she was.

"There — there — *mais voyons!*" I exclaimed in a vain effort to stop her tears — "*mais voyons!* Come, you must not cry like that." Little by little she ceased crying, until her sobbing gave way to brave little hiccoughs, then, at length, she opened her eyes.

"Suzette," I whispered — the thought flashing through my mind, "is it possible that *you* love Monsieur Tanrade?"

I saw her strong little body tremble: "No, monsieur," she breathed, and the tears fell afresh.

"Tell me the truth, Suzette."

"I have told monsieur the — the — truth," she stammered bravely with a fresh effort to strangle her sobs.

"You do not love Monsieur Tanrade, my child?"

"No, monsieur — I — I — was a little fool to have cried. It was stronger than I — the news. The marriage is so gay, monsieur — it is so easy for some."

"Ah — then you do love some one?"

"*Oui*, monsieur —" and her eyes looked up into mine.

"Who?"

"Gaston, monsieur — as always."

"Gaston, eh! the little soldier I lodged during the manœuvres — the little trombonist whom the general swore he would put in jail for missing his train. *Sapristi!* I had forgotten him — and you wish to marry him, Suzette?"

She nodded mutely in assent, then with a hopeless little sigh she added: "*Hélas* — it is not easy — when one has nothing one must work hard and wait — *Ah, mon Dieu!*"

"Sit down, my little one," I said. "I have

something serious to think over." She did as I bade her, seating herself in silence before the fire. I have never regarded Suzette as a servant — she has always been to me more like a child whom I was responsible for. What would my house abandoned by the marsh have been without her cheeriness, and her devotion, I thought, and what would it be when she was gone? No other Suzette would ever be like her — and her cooking would vanish with the rest. *Diable!* these little marriages play the devil with us at times. And yet, if any one deserved to be happy it was Suzette. I realized too, all that her going would mean to me, and moreover that her devotion to her master was such that if I should say "stay" she would have stayed on quite as if her own father had counselled her.

As I turned toward her sitting humbly in the chair, I saw she was again struggling to keep back her tears. It was high time for me to speak.

I seated myself beside her upon the arm of the chair and took her warm little hands in mine.

"You shall marry your Gaston, Suzette,"
I said, "and you shall have enough to marry
on even if I have to sell the big field and the
cow that goes with it."

She started, trembling violently, then gave
a little gasp of joy.

"Oh, monsieur! and it is true?" she cried
eagerly.

"Yes, my child — there shall be two weddings
in Pont du Sable!   Now run and tell Monsieur
le Curé."

Monsieur le Curé ran too, when he heard
the news — straight to my house abandoned,
by the short cut back of the village.

"*Eh bien!   Eh bien!*" he exclaimed as he
burst into my den, his keen eyes shining. "It is
too good to be true — and not a word to us
about it until now! *Ah, les rosses!   Ah, les
rosses!*" he repeated with a broad grin of
delight as he eagerly read Tanrade's letter,
telling him that the banns were published; that
he was to marry them in the little gray church
with the new bells and that but ten days

remained before the wedding. He began pacing the floor, his hands clasped behind him — a habit he had when he was very happy.

"And Suzette?" I asked, "has she told you?"

"Yes," he returned with a nod. "She is a good child — she deserves to be happy." Then he stopped and inquired seriously — "What will you do without her?"

"One must not be selfish," I replied with a helpless shrug. "Suzette has earned it — so has Tanrade. It was his unfinished opera that was in the way: Alice was clever."

He crossed to where I stood and laid his hand on my shoulder, and though he did not open his lips I knew what was passing in his mind.

"Charity to all," he said softly at length. "It is so good to make others happy! Courage, *mon petit* — the price we pay for love, devotion — friendship, is always a heavy one." Suddenly his face lighted up. "Have you any idea?" he exclaimed, "how much there is to do and how little time to do it in? Let us prepare!"

And thus began the busiest week the house

abandoned had ever known, beginning with the curé and I restocking the garret with dry wood while Suzette worked ferociously at house cleaning, and every detail of the wedding break-fast was planned and arranged for — no easy problem in my lost village in midwinter. If there was a good fish to be had out of the sea we knew we could rely on Marianne to get it. Even the old fisherman, Varnet, went off with fresh courage in search for clams and good Madame Vinet opened her heart and her wine cellar.

It was the curé who knew well a certain dozen of rare burgundy that had lain snug beneath the stairs of Madame Vinet's small café — a vintage the good soul had come into possession of the first year of her own marriage and which she ceded to me for the ridiculously low price of twenty sous the bottle, precisely what it had cost her in her youth.

It is over, and I am alone by my fire.

As I look back on to-day — their wedding day — it seems as if I had been living through some happy dream that has vanished only too quickly and out of which I recall dimly but half its incidents.

That was a merry procession of old friends that marched to the ruddy mayor's where there was the civil marriage and some madeira, and so on to the little gray church where Monsieur le Curé was waiting — that musty old church in which the tall candles burned and Monsieur le Curé's voice sounded so grave and clear. And we sat together, the good old general and I, and in front of us were Alice's old friend Germaine, chic and pretty in her sables, and Blondel, who had left his unfinished editorial and driven hard to be present, and beside him in the worn pew sat the Marquis and Marquise de Clamard, and the rest of the worn pews were filled with fisherfolk and Marianne sat on my left, and old Père Varnet with Suzette beyond him — and every one's eyes were upon Alice and Tanrade, for they were good to look upon. And it was over quickly, and I was glad of it, for the candle flames had begun to form halos before my eyes.

And so we went on singing through the village amid the booming of shotguns in honour of the newly wed, to the house abandoned. And all the while the new bells that Alice had so generously regiven rang lustily from the gray belfry — rang clear — rang out after us, all the way back to the house abandoned and were still ringing when we sat down to our jolly break-fast.

"Let them ring!" cried the curé. "I have two old salts of the sea taking turns at the rope," he confided in my ear. "Ring on!" he cried aloud, as we lifted our glasses to the bride — "Ring loud — that the good God may hear!"

And how lovely the room looked, for the table was a mass of roses fresh from Paris, and the walls and ceiling were green with mistletoe and holly. Moreover, the old room was warm with the hearts of friends and the cheer from blazing logs that crackled merrily up the black-ened throat of my chimney. And there were kisses with this feast that came from the heart; and sound red wine that went to it. And later, the courtyard was filled with villagers come to

congratulate and to drink the health of the
bride and groom.

They are gone.

And the thrice-happy Suzette is dreaming
of her own wedding to come, for it is long past
midnight and I am alone with my wise old cat —
"The Essence of Selfishness," and my good
and faithful spaniel whom I call "Mr. Bear,"
for he looks like a young cinnamon, all save
his ears. If poor de Savignac were alive he
would hardly recognize the little spaniel puppy he
gave me, he has grown so. He has crept into my
arms, big as he is, awakening jealousy in "The
Essence of Selfishness" — for she hates him —
besides, we have taken her favourite chair. Poor
Mr. Bear — who never troubles her ——

"And *you* — beast whom I love — another
hiss out of you, another flattening of your ears
close to your skull, and you go straight to bed.
There will be no Suzette to put you there soon,
and there is now no Alice, nor Tanrade to spoil
you. They are gone, pussy kit."

One o'clock — and the fire in embers.

I rose and Mr. Bear followed me out into the garden. The land lay still and cold under millions of stars. High above my chimney came faintly the "Honk, honk," of a flock of geese.

I closed my door, bolted the inner shutter, lighted my candle and motioned to Mr. Bear. The Essence of Selfishness was first on the creaky stairs. She paused half way up to let Mr. Bear pass, her ears again flat to her skull. Then I took them both to my room where they slept in opposite corners.

Lost village by the tawny marsh. Lost village, indeed, to-night! in which were hearts I loved, good comrades and sound red wine — Hark! the rush of wings. I must be up at dawn. It will help me forget —— Sleep well, Mr. Bear!

THE END